McCallister Chronicles

Kouenza and the King

Illustrated & Extended Edition
Black & White Printing

Written by:
A.P. Schreckenberger

Creative Content Support:
J.M. Harrison

Featured Artist:
"Raden" William Anugerah
http://radenwa.deviantart.com

Other Illustrations by:
Raven Cruz
J.M. Harrison
Lauren 'Ookii-Chan' MB
A.P. Schreckenberger

www.cfxt.com

Testimonials & Dedications

This is MC! Ocular annuli? You son of a bitch...~ Derrick Brace

One of the best works of literature I've read in many years. ~ Brian Campbell

Spectacular! Can't put it down! ~ Robin Martin

There are numerous people that should be thanked for helping me finish Kouenza and the King.

Luky, you told me to write… or else.

Ash, you've always been a source of encouragement.

Mom & Dad, you've always been listed in the *Friends and Family* section, but you deserve special props for never hindering my creative side.

Matt and Trisch, all I can say to you is *chka shemona eh hee hee!*

Derrick, with this book, we were able to discuss things on an intellectual plateau that we had not reached before.

WAFFLES, thank you for the fanart and support!

Raden, thank you for all the hard work you put into making the story come alive with your illustrations.

Come fair maidens, noble men, poor boys, and meager girls
Gather 'round and hear my word
Dedicated to a fictional world
Born from a sword and a holy cross
Affixed by the bindings of dawn and night

Listen to a story that all hold dear
For love, chaos, and even fear
Drive us towards what we must understand
After years of wait, the symphony will finally play its hand...
Night Suite in A Minor.

McCallister Chronicles

Based on J.M. Harrison's
Cartheim's Cross

A.P. Schreckenberger

Night Suite

Kouenza and the King
Book 1 – Episode 1

Confetti spilled across the city of Cartheim as chants arose from the crowds of people that poured onto the streets. Years of war with the neighboring province of Tistal had finally come to an end, and for the first time in almost two decades, citizens of the two realms gathered for a feast of celebration. Security personnel pushed commoners from the main road as the honor guard escorted the King of Tistal, Ereint de Marrok, and his daughter to the ceremony.

A pair of enchanted grayish-blue eyes stared at the mysterious writing that decorated the dark stone faces of the obelisk that dwarfed the town's square. The young princess continued to peer skyward as strange feelings plucked the strings of her heart and began a symphony that had not played for a generation. "Lukainy," her father roared after he snatched the ten-year-old from her trance, "greet your hosts properly." A smile appeared through his deep brown beard as a hand ventured to brush strands of blond hair from Luky's stunned face.

"Yes, Father," she replied, taking hold of the frills of her white gown and promptly giving an elegant curtsy to the present members of Cartheim's nobility. "It's a pleasure to meet you," she spoke as she acutely scrutinized all those in attendance. With her king satisfied, the royal returned her gaze to the stele as the hidden conductor's whisper drifted through her mind – *Lutti*.

"Damn guards," a peasant muttered as he stealthily darted down the alleyways. A tattered brown robe fluttered behind the child while fists eagerly punched through the wind. "I heard that the Princess of Tistal would be here, and I want to see her!" He dawdled with fanciful reveries that magically merged his life of thievery and haplessness with that of elegance and wealth. He pictured a sleek silhouette sewn into the fabric of his consciousness and fought to unmask the elusive image behind her shadow.[1]

Unfortunately, a redheaded knight yanked the youth from his imagination as he blocked the zigzagging detour and forced the brown-eyed orphan into a futile scramble. With ease, the soldier intercepted the minor and flattened his unkempt black hair with a massive palm strong enough to lift him from the ground. "Wing," the voice boomed as beady, maroon irides oppressed the child's widened gaze, "I thought I told you that you could not get close."

"Piss off, Kit!" Wing yelled before the paladin gripped his wrist and shoved him into one of the alley walls.

"I can do a lot of things for you brat," he growled and stared at the emblem tattooed onto the boy's right hand, "but I cannot possibly allow a branded kid access to the Tistalian convoy. The king would have me punished straight away; would you really want that?"

Waves of relaxation accompanied an amber tint that seeped onto Wing's oculars while he waited for Kit to lower his guard. "You want punishment?" Wing grunted as the insole of his leather-wrapped foot ripped through the gap between Kit's legs. He scowled as the knight's grasp broke, and in an instant, he felt the firm cobblestone path press against the soles of his raggedy shoes. "Sorry," the youth mumbled after dashing onto the road. His heart pounded as a voice nipped at his mind's ear – *Trigger* – and his legs carried him as fast as they could in search of the girl that he had to meet.

"What is a peasant doing on the court?" one of the honor guard shouted when Wing sprinted to the obelisk.

On the other side of the monument, Luka stood with her hands tenderly rubbing the stone. Although this was her first time in Cartheim, a feeling lingered that she had already been there. She could hear murmurs in her mind as she rounded the corner, her fingers exploring the rough surface while emotions from a forgotten dream bubbled into her soul.

"I have to meet her; I don't know why but I have to meet her!" Wing yelled when his palm collided with the monument.

"Stop!" the commander called, but Wing did not listen. Something drove him forward and continuously told him that things were not right. Brown orbs met the lightest shade of blue as he rounded the corner, and two worlds collided as two hearts had done long ago.

"Arrow!" was all Wing heard before a blinding light engulfed the square. The scratchy fabric of a hilt pressed against his palm, and the steel of a sword deflected the tip meant for the princess.

"Daizer," Kit muttered as he peered from the alleyway. His stare locked on the blade that had appeared from the void and chosen a pauper as its master. "It can't be that *that* kid is really him."

"Assassin on the rooftop!" another guard cried while Wing threw his other arm around Luky.

"I've found you," Wing whispered as an arrow dug into his back, his view of her shocked eyes fading to darkness. "I have finally found you."

*   *   *

"Wing, Wing, Wing!" Marrok shouted as she yanked the blanket from his bed. "Damn servant boy! Get up!"

Wing opened his eyes and looked at her with a groggy stare. "Eh, Luky, what are you doing here?" He grunted, sat up, and slowly rubbed his palpebrae, pausing only to look at his noble partner and her wardrobe of the day. In the months since they had started school, she tossed aside the elegant gowns that had defined her childhood and adopted loose blouses and short skirts of various shades of blue. "It's not fair to wake me up like that just so you can peek at my boxers, and you know how I am when I don't get enough sl...whoa!" His cheeks reddened as she tackled him into the bed with a giggle.

"Seven years have passed, and you haven't changed a bit. I don't give a damn about what you happen to be wearing. You should know by now that I woke you up because I missed the fire in your eyes."

"L-L-Luky," he stuttered when she pressed into his chest, her lips drifting closer and closer until they softly embraced his own. Her sweet, flowery scent filled the air as he took a breath before her tender kiss retook him, and he jerked from the silky hands that pressed delicately into his shoulders.

"Turn over," Luka mumbled as she pulled away, her gray eyes narrowing in time with the knees that pressed gently into his sides.

"You don't have to do it every single day," he replied quietly during a warming embrace.

"And you don't have to fight it every single day," she retorted with a leer. "Now turn the fuck over or I will make you turn the fuck over!"

Wing shrugged and peered into her orbs as a grin snuck onto his face from the corner of his lips. "Princess," he replied while his fingertips continued to play with her cheeks, "you may be royalty, but do you really have the strength to make me do anything?"

Lukainy's sharp glare continued as she bit at one of his thumbs and responded, "If you close your eyes, then maybe I will let you find out." She slid towards the foot of the bed as Wing's eyelids slowly rolled over the flickering ochre that lined his pupils. "Good boy," she smirked before turning him over with a yank of his ankles. In an instant, she had pinned him on his stomach, had his wrists tightly bound behind his back, and had his ankles locked together. "You always forget that knights serve the royal family and that you are still a knight in training." Delicately she rubbed the back of his right hand, feeling the tattoos that branded him as a peasant and personal guard.

Her soft cores gazed at a cross-shaped scar to the right of his spine, and after a moment of hesitation, she kissed it. "It's the only cross to which I can pray," Lukainy said before her teeth brushed against his nape and sent shivers through Wing's body. "I love you." Her hand reached into her blouse as she took another bite and listened to the moans that began to pour from his lungs. "Don't take that for granted," she whispered.

Wing blushed as a blindfold covered his oculars and felt his heart pound from her touch. "I love you too," he responded with a shyness in his voice to which Luky clung.

"Then tell me again," Lukainy commanded as her arms wrapped around his waist.

"I love you," he admitted while trembling from yet another nip. "I love you more than anything, and I'll always be here to protect you."

"I don't think you will be doing any protecting like that," Kit interrupted as he burst through the door. His eyes targeted Wing's blood-red cheeks as Marrok sighed at the captain.

"I'm not done with him yet," the princess cried. "Don't you knock?" She spotted someone standing behind the officer: a scrawny silver-haired boy with a sheepish look on his face and a kind presence about him. "And Dai!" Luka wailed, "I would not expect this intrusion from you!"

"Sorry, milady," he replied while the aristocrat continued her tirade.

"Well hurry it up already," Kit ordered, pushing Dai into the hall and leading him down the palace corridor. "Get changed," he mumbled to the boy, "because, once those two are done, we shall begin today's training."

"Is it really okay to have them waste that much time?" Dai asked when he halted in front of a small wooden door. The dry draft from the small alcove caused a smile to creep across Dai's lips, for he anticipated the escape from the damp pathway and the walls that glistened under candlelight. However, Kit remained silent through the boy's budding joy, and his stern expression yielded the answer to Dai's question.

Back in the bedroom, Luky ran her fingernails up and down Wing's sides, her eyes watching keenly as he shivered to her touch. "What should I do to you now?" she asked before pressing her nose into his soft, black hair to feast on the aromas of sweat and man. Droplets fled from his skin to the mark of royalty, and the princess did everything within her power to squeeze any part of Wing that she could. "Maybe I'll make you scream or wail my name until the whole palace hears you." She pressed forward and smirked at the sheepish smile that ensnared his coaxing lips. "You'd like that, wouldn't you slave?" Lukainy asked when she could feel his body quiver with excitement. She stood up and smacked his ass, laughing as she left her submissive vassal to fend for himself against the tyrants of teasing agony.

"Luky!!!" he roared; of course, the whole castle heard him. [2]

"Dammit," Wing grumbled as he stomped down the hall in a vibrant silver and gold armor suit. The juts of metal ejected rays that outshined their dim candlelight sources, but the knight's mood was hardly as beaming. "Leaving me like that is absolutely absurd," Wing pouted before his steel boot pried the door to Dai's room. He grinned when he saw his sword waiting, its white cloth-wrapped hilt and soul-forged blade bathing the small space with waves of starry gray. "Kit told you to change back, didn't he?" Wing asked while taking hold of the sword. "I guess that means we had better get to work and own those stuck up Academy jerks."

"I hope you are not talking about me," a person called from the hallway as a pair of green eyes appeared from behind the door.

"Hey D," Wing replied, stepping from the room with a sigh before eyeing the tall, muscular and dusk-blond man. "Going with the full noble threads today?"

"I need to impress the ladies, bro," Derrick replied as he showed off the attire. Despite the pageantry, the myrtle garments and leather-clad iron sheets cloaked a dependable man worthy of Wing's trust. The other members of the social elite were arrogant, cynical, and pompous; they would probably do better as circus masters than as Knights of the Royal Order. "Speaking of ladies, I heard that Luka pulled another number on you this morning," D chuckled while the pair walked down the hall. "You need to watch out for that because the others will bring it up and make you the laughingstock again."

"That's fine," Wing interrupted, swinging Daizer over his shoulder. "You know better than anyone that their dignity will blind them from defeating me. In fact, there are only four people at this school that I enjoy sparring."

"And who would those four people be?" Derrick asked, clicking his own sword against one of his armored boots.

"Kit, Luky, you," Wing paused as he pushed open the door to the courtyard, "and Dai." He squinted at the band of robed aristocrats that occupied the center of the field and grunted at their absurd babbling before clinging to the brick that outlined the space. "Go ahead," he mumbled to Derrick. "You'll get branded if you stay with me for too long."

"Hurry up, Alsyne," one of the trainees shouted, "or you will become diseased."

"God, they are ridiculous," Derrick complained as he strode towards the lawn. "Take it easy, McCallister. Hopefully today, we will get to spar."

"Alsyne!" a brunette wailed. Her slender arms embraced their target while a satisfied smile transformed her countenance. "I'm glad you got away from the filth." Her blue irides beamed as she gazed into his ocean-deep cores of green.

"Amora," Derrick replied with little emotion. The girl squealed to her name and tightened her grip on Alsyne's robes. "There is work to be done," he continued prior to stepping from her grasp. "Now is not the time or the place for affections to be displayed."

"That is right, sister," another trainee blurted when his hands wrapped around Amora's shoulders. "We are all – or almost all – here to become honorable knights of the kingdom." The man pressed his curly blond locks into his sister's cheeks before pulling away. "Alsyne can share his affections with you after we have our sparring matches."

"Ashton," Derrick mumbled to the boy before his stare set on Wing, "do not underestimate the nobility that lurks among us."

"Typical," Kit whispered when he stepped into the courtyard. "The brats are clustered together, and the peasant is alone on the sidelines." The captain sighed while his sight drifted from the tower-keep to the cobblestone archways that served as the boundaries of his schooling grounds. His ears remained open to the voice of fate, whose gentle melody played in the soothing breeze. "Today," he shouted to the class upon reaching a decision, "our first match will be between Derrick von Alsyne and Wing McCallister."

Wing pushed off the keep wall and gripped Daizer as a fang appeared from behind his lip. Derrick parted the aristocrats when he stepped towards Wing with an equally appeased smirk and pulled his broadsword from its holster. "Eh, Wing," Alsyne said, "it seems that the stars aligned for us."

Grass crunched in tympanic time with Wing's rush forward, and his blade stood ready to meet the advance of the rapidly charging Alsyne. *Upper left*, Wing heard Daizer call before the cacophony of clashing steel pierced the air. The two paused just long enough to let waves of green crash against a beach of amber. *He has a soul-forge too*, Daizer commented before Wing leapt back and dug his feet into the supple ground.[3]

"I see," Wing said, pointing Daizer directly at Derrick. "You have been holding out on me, which means this fight is going to be all the more interesting."

From below, Daizer whispered before Derrick's blade once again clashed with Wing's razor. Dust jetted into the air with each jolt and swipe as sweat dripped between skin and armor. *He's strong*, the sword spoke after Wing grunted from another block, *but you are wearing him down Wing.*

"No Dai," Wing replied, feeling the heat pour from his muscles into the tightly fitted armor. "Derrick is not like the others, for he is not blinded by society." Wing lurched forward and made an impressive swing with his blade. "Alsyne is a worthy opponent!"

Derrick smiled when his sword accented the final collision with Daizer. Both huffed as the piece hung in a prolonged fermata, and Kit, the conductor, soon after concluded the match as per time regulations. "What were your flaws?" he asked the pair as they lowered their swords.

"A noble fought a peasant," Ashton interrupted snobbishly before Kit shot the student a demonic glare.

"Stamina," Derrick commented, his green eyes once again peering into Wing's amber orbs. "There was nothing wrong with Wing's form nor did he find anything wrong with mine. It was just a matter of exhaustion, and that is the way that most battles end when two opponents of equal skill meet on the field of war."

No matter how real the battle may have been, Luky's heart still pounded with worry after she watched the engagement. "Why are you not down there with him?" an older woman said upon entering the tower's small chamber. Her faded blond hair was tied in an elegant bun that gripped the back of her head, her light purple dress appeared as an ocean of fabric that swelled and dipped with each step, and her soft chestnut irides cast a comforting tide that flooded the princess's soul.

"Mother," Luka replied, turning around to graciously greet Her Majesty. "I am sorry, but I do not join Wing unless he absolutely needs me."

"He always needs you," she said, walking to the window pane to glance at the boy of common birth that continued to climb the ranks. "Go to him."

"As you wish," Luky replied with a bow before frantically running down the stairs to the courtyard.

Meanwhile, the Queen of Tistal stood with her hand pressed to the thin plane of glass. Her hazel orbs kept their sights locked onto Wing and Derrick as a voice within her continued to spin the tale of a distant past. "It seems that your brothers have returned, Harmony."

Book 1 – Episode 2

Wing gripped Daizer's sheath and hunched forward when Luky leapt onto his back. "You worried me," she exclaimed, her eyes coldly glancing at Derrick.

"Feel free to take him away," Ashton interjected as he fidgeted with his flawless locks. "It's not like we need…"

Derrick stomped past Ashton's side, his metal-encased fist pounding the boy's jaw. "Stay your tongue," Alsyne roared before his sharp leer bit into the fallen Hunter, "or I shall remove it for you."

"What are you doing, Alsyne?" Ashton spat, blood trickling from his nose and mouth. "Are you siding with a peasant over a noble? The court will have your rank and title for this! You had better believe that my father will not…" He grunted when Derrick planted a boot on his face and pressed it into the grass strewn mud.

"Your father will not do anything," D retorted, "because a noble knows when to shut his mouth. The last time I checked, McCallister defeated you in a fair battle, which means that the peasant is your better." He turned to Amora, who stood awestruck throughout the confrontation until Derrick peered into her soul with his enchanting eyes. "Please take care of your brother and try to help him understand his proper place in society. Nobles do not exist to make fun of peasants; they exist to guide and protect those less fortunate than ourselves."

"Amora," Kit interrupted after stepping into the fray, "take your brother to the medical ward, please. I normally would punish anyone for participating in an unsanctioned fight, but Derrick is correct. Ashton, your arrogance will lead to your downfall." The knight's soft gaze drifted to Wing and Luka, who carried on a bickering match of their own in the background. "He may not have status now, but had his parents survived the Battle of Cartheim…" Kit paused and decided to change the subject entirely. "You could learn from him if you were not blinded by your own ambition."

"What the hell do you know?" Ashton bit as Amora led her shaken brother inside. "You cannot possibly understand the pressures we face."

"I don't like it when you fight alone!" Luky roared before taking a bite at Wing's ear. Her legs were wrapped tight around his chest, and her arms clung to his neck during the attack.

"Princess, what is wrong with you?" Wing cried, tears forming in his canthi as she bit down harder. "I am in the middle of a class; you can't be doing this right now. You need to be training too!"

"I need to be training?" she quipped, hopping off his back. "Then my training partner will be you!" Her gray orbs appeared ecstatic as she reached into her blouse and retrieved a long whip that had been tied around her waist.

"Oh shit," Wing muttered when he jumped back to a safer distance. "Luky, please be a bit more rational…" He gasped as the whip coiled around his neck. *She has gotten better,* Wing thought, his eyes widening with each step Marrok took to close the gap between them.

"You will be fighting with me, idiot," she whispered while her hands pressed against his armor. "Remember though, I am the only one allowed to hurt you." She smiled at Wing's blush before turning her head to face Kit. "Take Wing's sword inside and bring out the training weapons," she ordered. "I want a physical fight. And while you are at it, tell Dai to come and participate. I know my baby wants an opponent with class."

"Are you up for another round already?" Derrick asked, stepping up to Wing with an exhausted yawn. "I think I am going to head back to my room and get some rest. There is no point staying out here to watch the pansies fail miserably."

"Does it look like I have much of a choice?" Wing replied quietly while Luky forced Kit inside with Daizer. "She can get a little…"

Wing felt clumps of dirt pound against his shins as Luka appeared from a cloud of dust and gripped his ear with a growl. "I heard that," she grumbled, darkness drenching her suddenly coarse voice, "and trust me when I say that you will be paying for it later. If you are going to be fighting, then I am going to be fighting with you, partner. Get it? Got it? Good!"

Derrick laughed and turned towards the door. "Take it easy, Wing," he mumbled as his glance shifted to Luky. "Don't be too rough on him, milady. He exists only to protect you."

Memories crept from the past's exiled penumbra into Lukainy's consciousness during Derrick's departure. His noble robes of dark green made her boil over the flames of a distant fear that threatened the purpose and the manifestation of her love. Softly, her fingers touched the whip still wrapped around Wing's neck, and soon after, she leaned forward to deliver unto him a sacred kiss. "Promise me," she spoke into his ear, "that you will never fight without me."

Burgundy awnings hung over the stained glass windows that decorated Alsyne's elegant chamber. "What do you think, Lara?" he said before tossing his broadsword onto a king-sized, pillow-top mattress.

Derrick gazed at the beautiful woman that had appeared from hidden catacombs of pounded steel. Her dark oculars seemed like voids that cried out to him with a siren's call, and her sculpted body was covered by addictively thin, yet carefully placed strips of leather. "I think that Dai is cute," she responded with a lick of her lips and with a flick of her flowing black hair. "I also think that Wing houses Trigger's psyche." She rose from the bed and stepped towards Alsyne seductively before placing her hand on his shoulder. "You do what you need to do, Defy," Lara cooed while staring into his charming eyes. "In the meantime, I am going to take the opportunity to play with that metal hunk. I am curious to see what he'll look like in his other form."

Wing and Luky stood waiting when the doors opened and Dai emerged. Leather armor clung to his torso, and gleaming steel boots pressed into the ground with every step that he took. The girls in the courtyard swooned at his presence, his heavenly silver hair, and his deep purple orbs that froze weaker hearts in their places. "Wing," Dai said, "I heard that you wanted to see me. Why wake a noble from his slumber?"

He plays the part well, Wing thought to himself before pointing at his sword in disguise. "Alsyne thinks that I need to work on my stamina, and who better to fight than the Academy's endurance legend?" During their first months in the Palace Academy, Wing and Dai had worked to create an alter ego for the soul-forge. McCallister presumed that if he leaked his blade's true identity, collectors, thieves, and nobles would bring unnecessary distractions to the campus. Thus, Dai of Cartheim came to be the noblest of nobles, the piece of Wing that the upper-class unwittingly admired, and the perfect training partner.

"You cannot possibly defeat me when it comes to stamina, McCallister," Dai responded while his sights wandered to the excited students. "But I admire your courage and will accept your challenge. I take it that Princess Lukainy will be joining you, and I accept those odds as well."

"Not so fast," Lara interrupted upon stepping from the palace, her light leather wares prompting the male students in attendance to gape. "So it's you," she said while gripping Dai's arm. "I have a whip too. If you let me join, then I'll show you how it works."

"You're…" Dai began, but he was quickly interrupted by Lara's finger pressing into his lips.

"Don't ruin the fun," Lara replied teasingly, her voice getting quiet as she pushed her body against his chest. "I won't harm the girl, but I would like to play with that master of yours." She felt Dai shiver and giggled quietly while giving his cheek a gentle kiss. "If I enjoy the fight with him, I will repay you in the best way I know how; but if you spoil my opportunity, I'll let out your little secret." Lara pondered the power of her feminine persuasion and purred at how easily she manipulated the situation; not only would she be able to gauge Wing's abilities, but she would also get the chance to fight with Dai.

However, the male blade scowled and turned his cheek away from Wing and Luka. Her forwardness and audacity shocked him into an ever-deepening blush, but before he committed to anything, he had to make sure that she would not endanger his comrades. "If you don't hurt them," he spoke under his breath, "then I have no objections."

"I won't hurt them," Lara commented while dragging her hand up Dai's armor, "much. Just don't get in the way of what needs to be done."

"Dai!" Wing shouted. "What the hell is going on over there, and who the heck is she?"

"I'm Lara, Lara von Alsyne," she replied, pushing Dai away before a whip appeared in her right hand. "I see that Lukainy enjoys whips, so I decided to join in on the fun. I hope you don't mind Wing, and don't worry, I'd much rather make you scream than make a lady of royalty."

Luky cracked her whip against the ground and glared with a fire in her eyes. "What does that mean!?" she roared before ripping up thickets of dirt with another sharp crack. "I am not a pushover…"

Lara explained, "Please do not misunderstand. I am not questioning your abilities or your weapon skills; I would just rather make the knight howl in agony than listen to the high-pitched squeal of a little girl."

"Bitch," Marrok shouted, watching in disgust as the female Alsyne jumped out of the range of her first attack.

"Feisty, aren't we?" In the blink of an eye, Lara had her whip wrapped around Wing's neck, its serrated grip digging into his flesh as she pulled it tight. "I'll make a deal with you, Princess. Each time that you attack me, I get to tear off a little piece of him."

Wing gripped the rope and relaxed the pull on his body before he jerked the cord to throw off Lara's balance. Blood seeped from his wounds as McCallister lunged forward, and his mind tinkered with the circumstances of Lara's arrival and participation. *It's likely that she knows his secret,* he thought, factoring in Dai's present neutrality, *which means that she is D's soul-forge.* "I won't fight a girl one-on-one," he roared, blazing past Lara to bring his only hope into the confrontation.

"I think not," she mumbled, regaining control of her whip after Wing's maneuver. With a snap of the wrist, she launched the weapon at Luky and grinned at the resulting scream. The high-pitched cry drilled into Wing's ears and gripped his heart. Its beat intensified as Wing dug his foot into the ground and reversed course; he would not allow the princess to become the victim of the battle, and before the second crack descended from the sky at the speed of sound, he was there to take the hit. "You are a knight after all," Lara giggled and watched amusedly as Wing became Luka's shield.

"Don't underestimate me!" Lukainy yelled after flinging her whip around Wing's body. She had sent her weapon on the perfect arc to strike Lara on the cheek, but Dai jumped forward to catch the rope with his hand.

"You're overdoing it," Dai warned prior to charging the pair. His fist dug into the metal armor encasing Wing's torso and cracked the fine gear before the paladin could defend with his bloodied arms. "It's over," Dai said, hoping to end the fight before further damage could be done, but Lara utilized the opening to launch an assault on the unguarded noble. Cracks echoed throughout the courtyard as Luky counterattacked with her own whip and charged the metal soul.

"I told you," Alsyne replied when her lash broke apart the pieces of Wing's ruined armor and gnawed his chest. "Every time you attack me, I will take a piece of his flesh as a souvenir." She licked her canine fang and looked at the distraught royal. "Though, if he wants to give me something of greater value, then I might be inclined to reconsider." Lara smacked the whip across Wing's cheek and watched him fall into slowly forming creeks of blood. "Are you nothing without your sword?" she asked, her gaze focusing on the fallen trainee. "Why should a blade serve you if you cannot serve yourself or fulfill any purpose?"

"That's enough," Dai interrupted, stepping between Lara and Wing.

"Is it?" she replied, digging the head of her serpent into the ground. "You've been soft with them. They don't even know the first goddamn thing about real fighting. I came all this way to see it, and I will not let you interfere." Lara's whip slithered through the air following a thunderous snap of the girl's wrist, and the tip hissed throughout its flight towards Luky. Dai's eyes widened as he felt a rush of heat engulf his back. The invisible inferno chilled him to the metallic bone, but before he could blink, it was gone. Instead, the heat stood before Luka, encased Wing's wine-stained flesh, and soared from his ochre oculars to dig into Lara's forged essence. Simultaneously, her snake of rope fell to pieces as a fleeting blue spark danced from Lukainy's whip.

"I told you," Marrok said, wrapping her free arm around Wing's chest. His blood coated her skin when she pulled him closer, and she could feel his pain as he quivered silently in her grasp. "He belongs to me."

Lara smiled and turned away without making a sound. She stood there for a moment, trying to think of the right words to say, but her thoughts remained fixed to one thing. *They can free Defy.* "Dai," she finally mumbled, "I would like to talk to you later if I could." Alsyne paused before her dark orbs gazed upon Wing and Luky. "Take good care of that man, Your Highness. I guess you are the only one that gets his goods." She smiled and departed, leaving the trio of fighters and the class in a state of confusion.

Wooden swords dropped to the grass when Kit gazed upon the puddles of Wing's blood that cluttered the courtyard. "Kit!" Luka wailed, tears streaking down her cheeks while she struggled to hold Wing's bludgeoned body. She heard his agony with every huff of breath, and her heart pulsed with ever-growing anxiety that fed off the trickles of life that dripped from his wounds. "Take him to my room," she commanded as Dai took hold of his master. "I want him in my bed!" Luky explained. "And I don't care what happens to it." She dashed into the castle and frantically searched for the medical supplies that could save his endangered life.

Derrick sat quietly by the fireplace in his stately bedroom and peered at the flickering green flames that danced about the hearth.

"Defy," a voice seemed to emanate from the fire, "what data have you collected?"

"General Conrad," Derrick sneered in response as his fists clenched with rage.

"Do not test me, Defy," Conrad replied. "I became the master of the Enchantment Flame, and by that contract, you serve me. Tell me what you have discovered."

Alsyne passionately hated Conrad; the man who had stolen his powers at the climax of the Great War, threatened to destroy the remnants of the first family, and sought to form a global empire was no better than a diseased rat. Yet long ago, Defy had been corrupted by the evil of the conniving fifth child and was forced to fight his brother in a grueling war for Cartheim. "There is no doubt that Trigger lies within the boy, but he has not yet discovered the true power of the Battle Flame."

"And what of Tistal's princess?" Conrad continued as the blaze licked the stone mantel.

"Princess Lukainy is Lutti's harbor, but she has not discovered her innate abilities either."

"Then I shall act as soon as possible," the general responded. "The Hapsburg 7th will cross the border of Tistal in three days. In the meantime, I shall give you enough power to complete one task for me. Place the King of Tistal under the spell of my flame and command him to send Wing to face my army alone. Order the girl to stay behind and incarcerate her if necessary. With the two of them separated, Trigger's shell will die, and Lutti will be mine to wed." Alsyne watched a spark jump from the hearth to his palm and felt the Enchantment Flame burn within him once again. "Don't get used to it," Conrad exclaimed. "I will warn you Defy; if you try to betray me, or if you fail in this task, I will use our connection to make you wither away."

"I know already," D replied. "Quit your whining and just let me do my job."

"This assignment is important, Defy," the general emphasized. "If your brother is taken out of the equation, my work can be completed with a lot less bloodshed. That's what you want, isn't it?"

Luky crashed through doors of her bedroom, glanced at the unconscious Wing, and snapped her head to the attentive Kit and Dai. "Thanks you two, now get out!" she roared and stomped to the bed, placing rope, a bowl of medicinal ointment, and a pile of bandages on the soft mattress. Her irides burned with a passionate blue fire as she gripped the cuffs of Wing's pants and yanked them off.

"Take good care of him, Your Majesty," Kit muttered before dragging Dai out of the room and closing the doors. His head pressed against the gate of oak, and he whispered with a sorrow-filled sigh, "You are the only one that can."

The princess gazed at the stripped Wing and pulled the rope into her hands before tying his wrists and ankles to the bedposts. "I wish I could do this under better circumstances," she commented as her hands clasped the bowl. "This may hurt a bit, baby," she continued, dipping a piece of cloth into the balm before stroking his scratched cheeks.

Wing's eyes shot open, and a gasp rushed past his lips. He struggled against the stinging that clenched his nerves, and his pupils dilated from the mounting confusion. "Lu-Lu," he stuttered when she straddled his waist and finally came into view.

"I'm sorry," she whimpered, tears swelling around her orbs. She pressed the cloth into the gouges that had chiseled his arms and listened to the painful grunts that constricted his lungs as well as the cacophonous teeth grinding that syncopated the sinful melody. The bedposts whined from the sharp plucks as Luky wrapped the ointment-coated fabric around Wing's marred neck.

"C-can't breathe," he gasped, continuing to squirm after Luky set the vessel and cloth aside. Eternity passed between the start and the end of a breath that the royal lady delivered to Wing's battered body. Her rosy lips embraced his parched pair as if the universe's existence depended upon a single kiss.

"We'll take a break," Lukainy cooed prior to bandaging the wounds that she had already treated. With her hands venturing to tame his wild hair, Luka observed the cuts covering her servant. The bleeding had finally stopped, although the princess remained wary of the situation. Until treated and bandaged, it remained possible for the fragile fermata that held his life to give way to an infectious tempo of suffering and demise. "I'm sorry for bringing you pain," she sobbed, her hand taking hold of the felt.

Pain scorched Wing's chest, cracks from the corners of the bed filled the air, and screams echoed throughout the chamber once Luky doctored the remaining gashes. She cried silently as spasms contorted her knight, and her hands trembled while she finished wrapping the final bandages around his torso. Her ears throbbed from the deafening wails that shattered the serenity of the escape; thus, the noble nestled her protector atop a sheet of life's wine and murmured messages of love to quell the sadistic demon that tore him apart.

"Stay with me," he panted repeatedly, his body gradually relaxing before their duet faded to black.

Book 1 – Episode 3

Dai stared at the ceiling of his tiny room, the straw bed beneath his human form providing little comfort to repress the pain. Wing's shrieks scratched at his distraught conscience and made him release a disappointed sigh. "I should have done more," he mumbled as a knock came from the door. He sat up when Lara entered the room and glared at her with his intrinsically soft, amethyst eyes. "What were you thinking?" he roared before she pressed her hand over his mouth.

"I'm sorry," she whispered. "I know I went too far, but you will understand soon enough. Please, keep it down, though; Defy must not find out about Wing's injuries, and he cannot know that I have come to speak with you in private."

"Why should I listen to you?" Dai snapped. "You nearly killed Wing. Did you see the blood pouring from his wounds?" He stopped and blushed when she sprawled him out on the bed.

"Shh," Lara replied upon resting her chin on Dai's shoulder. Strips of leather gripped into his skin as the female visitor moved into a straddling position. "I know you felt his inferno at the end of the match. You are not the only one who knows that Trigger's soul dwells within Wing, and I am sure that you have your own suspicions about Lukainy's gifts too. What's important is that Defy – the one you call Derrick von Alsyne – understands that Wing is merely a harbor for the First King of Cartheim and the Third Child of Aurora."

"Defy was the cause of the first war," Dai commented. "He was the one who sent Trigger to his grave and destroyed my father…"

"He wasn't the one…" Lara responded.

"No," Dai interrupted, sitting up with a foreboding scowl plastered to his face. "If you're Defy's blade, then I have no business listening to the foolishness coming from your mouth."

"You have to listen to me," she whimpered, pressing her head into his chest before driving him down to the straw. Dai began to sit up once again when he caught the tears pooling in her eyes. "Defy is not the bad guy," she cried. "There is another behind the scenes who manipulated everyone. His name is Conrad, and it is he who wields the Enchantment Flame as well as Derrick's life." She paused to wipe the puddles of salt water that gripped the bridge of her nose. "Wing is the only one who can save him."

Dai gulped and stared at the ceiling for a few seconds while her words scavenged through his mind's abundant pastures. *Her story is believable,* he thought, critically analyzing the tale and picking apart the consequences of their meeting. "I do remember my father mentioning something about an additional power in the war," he spoke quietly, "but you're going to have to offer something as proof. Especially after your handling of the fight today, I cannot trust you with the life of my comrades on word alone."

"I figured you would say something like that," she responded before kneeling above his waist. With reddened cheeks, she placed her hand upon the ribbon covering her breasts and plucked it off.

"Eh?" Dai exclaimed, blood pumping to his head as he spun onto his stomach and planted his face in the stalks. "You can't corrupt me with sex!" he shouted while her knees rubbed against his sides. Her fingernails brushed against the back of Dai's neck and sent ravaging shivers down his spine.

"If only I could," she murmured intimately. Lara giggled at Dai's shyness, at the way he wriggled beneath her, and at the way his head pressed deeper and deeper into the bed. *He's sweet,* she concluded; m*ost men would have tried something perverted by now.* Her hands caressed his cheeks, and her nose found its way into his supple silver hair. "Turn around," she said, taking in his cinnamon scent. "I am going to give you your request."

Dai turned his head slowly, revealing a wide purple ocular that timidly glanced upon Lara's sparkling physique. Candlelight reflected off her flawless skin and triggered waves of arousal that gripped Dai's brow and forced him to squint. He struggled to form comprehensible sentences and clenched his eyes shut when Lara gripped his shoulder and pushed him onto his back. A minute passed until his hand became blanketed in pulses of heat that wrapped his forged psyche in courage and lifted the dark mist that veiled his sight. Streams of crimson and argent trickled from a wound lodged between Lara's breasts, and Dai immediately sat up to care for her. "What are you doing?" he exclaimed, guiding the girl gently to the reeds before glancing at his palm.

"This is…" Dai began, observing a smooth, pebble-sized object while beams of emerald flared in the gaps between his fingers.

"My heart," Lara interrupted as she grew increasingly tired. "As long as you hold that, I can never attack you, Dai-kun." Peering into his concerned eyes, Lara found the spark of hope that would finally let her rest. She yawned and brushed his cheek lightly before mumbling, "I trust you. You're a good guy."[4]

The duet had faded to a rhythmic rustle that crept through the air with every snap Dai's boots made with the brick floor. His mind entrenched around the thoughts of Lara, who fell asleep in his locked abode upon delivering her proof with spirit attached. The thumping that infected Daizer's essence came not from his step, nor from her gift, but from the rushed beat that drove his own heart. To give up one's core, to a soul-forge, required more than trust alone; the act was a gesture of companionship, servitude, and love. Yet Dai's lightning pace through the halls of the palace only riled the thunderous question that rattled his thoughts: *to whom did she pledge her love?*

Regardless of the answer, Lara's actions told him that she was serious and that her story was true; thus, before he departed for Marrok's chamber, he tended Lara's injury, covered her with his noble robes, and shoved her gem into the pocket of his leather battle gear. However, the intentions bound to Dai's frantic tempo blinded him from the commotion that his appearance generated. Baffled students of rank gazed in awe upon the elite of the elite who marched through the palace corridors in training equipment, and Derrick von Alsyne was included on the list of enticed residents.

"Is something wrong with Dai, Charles?" Derrick asked upon stepping beside his brown-haired classmate.

The teen turned and glanced at Alsyne with gray orbs while his arms crossed beneath finely woven robes of black. "You never told me that one of your relatives attended the school," he replied in a coarse tone. "I am guessing that Dai is on his way to check on Lukainy and Wing; Lara really had fun torturing the two."

"Cousin," D spoke with a hushed whisper. "What happened?"

"Lara teamed up with Dai and whipped Wing to a bloody mess. I had my doubts about that peasant punk, but, after the way he defended the princess, I am starting to think that maybe we have been a little too hard on him."

Check it out, Conrad hissed telepathically, drowning out the second sentence of Charles's explanation. *If the boy is already injured, then I want you to eliminate him immediately.*

Touch was the first sense Wing regained as he rested in a realm of night. He could feel someone's soft warmth pour into his chest and remained content to float atop the sea of his inner self. Blue flames, however, broke the darkness of solitude and coaxed the drifter back to the dominion of the living. The tongues of vibrant turquoise took hold of his limbs and cradled his head over the midnight ocean that lurked below his suspended body. "She needs you," said a woman whose voice echoed throughout his amber-laced abyss.

"Luky!" Wing screamed as his eyes burst open. His arms and legs tugged at the ropes that bound him to the bed while his nose captured the girl's alluring scent. McCallister sighed and relaxed, giving in to the fingertips that gently gripped his shoulders.

"You're awake," Luka mumbled, her cheek resting on the bandages that covered Wing's torso. The blue shade that permeated her gray irides dripped onto the cloth wraps in a rain of tears that fell all the way to Wing's skin. "Why are you stupid?" she whined, her nails tightening the hold on the cadet as she gazed upon his shocked expression. "You didn't have to do that for me, idiot," the princess sniffled before the downpour spread to Wing's cheeks. "I told you not to get hurt…"

"Nothing hurts except watching you cry," Wing replied, staring at the watery spheres that crushed his heart.

"What are you talking about?" Lukainy shouted after she grabbed the ends of the gauze strips that were taped to her paladin's face. "That bitch whipped you until you passed out!" She yanked the wrappings from his flesh and froze. "What?" she questioned quietly while her hands tore the bandages from Wing's neck and chest. Blood stained the richly white sheets, brown scabs clung to the rough fabric that once held the teen together, but only his cross-shaped scar remained.

"Milady," Dai said upon entering the room, "I have some information." He paused and glanced at the blushing Wing, a smirk appearing on his face as he closed his eyes to respect his master's privacy. "It's true then," he spoke with a repressed giggle. "Your Highness, you are the reincarnation of Lutti d'Espoir."

"The Healing Flame," Luky responded while looking over her helpless protector. His declaration appeared to desert the bourns of truth, but Daizer was a shy boy tied to chivalric law, and the miraculous recovery of McCallister provided all the proof Luka desired. She turned back to the soul-forge and crawled off the bed before an aura of seriousness surged from the depths of her soul. "What is the news you bring, and where did you acquire it?"

Dai took a deep breath and lowered his head while tufts of his silver hair caught a chilling draft; he knew that the situation would be hard to explain to Luky, and he figured that Lara's involvement would only agitate her raging emotions. "Derrick…"

"Yo," Derrick interrupted upon thrusting open the door to Lukainy's room. Alsyne focused on Wing and completely missed the trembling shiver that rolled up the spine of the unnerved Dai. "I heard that my blade beat the crap out of you, but she actually showed interest in a guy for once, and I just could not forbid her the opportunity to meet Dai. I am sorry that I did not tell you earlier, but I am sure you know the reasons why wielders of special blades conceal that information."

Why the hell do people always barge in? Wing thought as he nodded. "Don't worry about it, D," McCallister replied while trying to break free from the binds. "As you can tell, the only thing hurt is my pride."

Derrick laughed and turned to the exit. "You look fine to me," he commented, a forced grin revealing a glimmering canine tooth. In reality, the laughter was Defy's pitiful attempt to escape the harsh jabs of Conrad's voice that continually stabbed his mind. "Pipe down," Alsyne muttered. "Your plot still unfolds, general. Wing got lucky this time; his injuries were not severe, and Luky and Daizer were both attending to him. You know that a rushed assassination attempt in those circumstances would probably backfire and pit both Cartheim and Tistal against the House of Hapsburg." *Go to the king* was the only response Defy received.

That was close, Dai thought. His anxiety feasted upon the damp air that poured into his artificial lungs as well as the mildew stench that gripped and twisted his olfactory senses. His bust filled with that state of medieval decay, and his lavender gaze grasped Marrok before the atmosphere recoiled from the exclamation, "Derrick is Defy!"

Luky sighed and planted her fists onto a large mahogany desk that decorated the corner of her room. Her hands ground the fine layer of dust that collected on the surface of the carved wood, and her pupils followed the curved metal lining of the window panes that opened her inner world to a universe of ornate green and sky blue. "You got that information from Lara, didn't you?" she bit back darkly, not waiting for an answer. "Why should I believe someone who bashed the person I love?"

"You should believe her because she knows about your flames!" Daizer retorted, his hand tightening its grip on Lara's heart. "I did not believe her either, but," he paused, "she gave me the core to her quintessence."

"I do not care," Luka roared, spinning around before she glimpsed at the star-like object resting in Dai's spread palm. Notes of emerald light orchestrated a silent symphony that fragmented the princess's rage, and the subtle plucks of Wing's voice that followed the optical masterpiece dulled her sharpened tongue.

"Luky," Wing said calmly, "if Lara gave her heart to Dai, then it means he can no longer be injured by her attacks." He paused and looked into the deep gray eyes that appeared to expand with every word he spoke. "It is the same as my oath to you; regardless of what happened earlier, Lara is probably telling the truth."

He's an idiot, Luky pondered, her nails digging into her palms under the force of an unnoticed anger. *He gets hurt and shrugs it off as if it means absolutely nothing.* The blue fire returned to her irides before she took a step towards the bed.

"However, Dai," Wing continued, his words failing to reach the deranged Lukainy, "if she wanted to billow our innate powers, and if she had that much information about us, then I do not see why she had to attack us in the severe manner that she did. I understand the sacrifice she made to prove her point to you, but until I talk to her myself, I have to remain somewhat skeptical."

"Wing," Marrok's demonic discourse shattered the tranquility as she gripped the boy's cheeks with her bloodied fingers. "She is a sadistic bitch," the riled noble roared, smacking Wing roughly before she jumped on top of him. "No one has the right to hurt you but me, no one has the right to protect you but me, and your flame exists for no one but me!" Her claw-like nails dug into his nape as she yanked his head from the bed and bit his lower lip in a kiss that dangled in an eternal fermata.

The princess shoved the stunned soldier back to the mattress. Her vibrant, brassy fanfare ignored the broken, delayed rumble that rolled from Wing's lips, for it favored the shocked purplish flare that gushed from Daizer's broadened stare. "If Lara wants to prove herself to someone," she growled, "then she can prove herself to me." Her palpebrae descended over the pair of cobalt-infected orbs before her hand ventured to the bedside nightstand. "In the meantime, you can store your prize in this," she continued, flicking a golden locket and chain to Dai with a snap of her wrist. "If you see her, send her, and I shall decide what to believe." Luka turned back to Wing and stroked him with an adventurous trailblazer. "Now beat it, Dai; I want some time with my knight."

Worn fingers massaged a kempt beard that had long ago turned white with age, and eyes willingly threw their sights upon scars of war that clung to the king's flesh like bloodthirsty leeches. Each one represented a chilling reminder of the augmented dissonance that once plagued his reign, but Ereint's leadership had eventually guided the realm back to tonic. His daughter had found love from an unlikely source, his kingdom had basked in peace for seven years, and little had since disturbed the gray serenity of his brick and mortar hall. On the throne, he sat, glistening under the assistance of candlelight and from the gold crown that contained his white mane.

"Your Highness!" a guard cried from the entryway, his nasally diction echoing off the forbidding walls. "Derrick von Alsyne of Cartheim has requested an audience with you."

Thick chestnut-colored robes fluttered when the king rose from his seat, and specks of dust hovered above the floor while riding the breve wind that wafted over the stone. "Send him," Ereint replied, his crisp sky-blue gaze meeting the entering Alsyne. "Lukainy is not giving you trouble again, is she?" Pearly canine teeth appeared from behind the king's ghostly mustache as he cracked a grin.

"No, King Ereint," Derrick replied, "but she is having her fun with Wing."

"Again?" Ereint sighed, smacking his forehead with his palm. "Those two are just impossible to control."

The weight crushing Defy's beating heart failed to hinder the laughter that departed his lips. He could feel his greened irides burn from the heat of enchantment – that coaxing, passionate flame that lured mere mortals into his spell and cursed his enslaved soul. "That is why I have come to see you," Alsyne replied, his voice deceptively slithering towards the mighty ruler.

The alluring timbre that latched onto Defy's sound sent Ereint stumbling back onto his throne. Goosebumps rose from his skin and pressed into the royal fabric as if little pieces of the monarch tried to avoid the chills that shook his body. Memories once at the tips of his fingers fell into the void of the forgotten, and fragmented thoughts filled the darkness left by the departing sanity. Ereint's chest heaved while he struggled to put words to the situation, but in his state of emptiness, he lost his muse. The only name that escaped the captured king was *Defy* coasting a repressed breeze.

Book 1 – Episode 4

Hate-filled hazel orbs glared at the looming hospital ceiling through parted bangs of blond. The chipped white paint that clung to the hardwood twisted Ashton's heart into a knot. Was he meant to become just a little flake that never contributed to the entire picture? Were Derrick's words true? Would he always live in Wing's unbreakable shadow? "Filthy slave," he sneered, glancing at his concerned sister before returning his attention to the emotionless structure. "He should not even be here; this is supposed to be an academy for knights destined to serve the royal line, and instead, we get the trash off the street. Why does Princess Lukainy believe that Wing could possibly serve her needs?"

"He's just a pet, Ashton," Amora replied lazily, for her mind continued to dwell on Derrick's harsh words towards her brother.

Maybe it's not worth the stress, she thought, resting her hand on Ashton's forehead while her ocean eyes glanced over the bruises that marred his cheek and eyebrow. However, the discontinuity between discourse and reality only split the girl's heart in twain when her thoughts of Alsyne collided with the black-tainted welts building beneath her brother's skin. "Focus on becoming better," Amora finally spoke, her thumb gently brushing her patient's cheek.

"How are you feeling Ashton?" Charles asked, emerging from the entryway while his robes lingered in his wake. "There are quite a few injuries today," he sighed. "It is becoming more and more tedious to make my rounds."

"How do you think I am feeling?" Hunter roared his response. "I got punted in the face by that bastard Alsyne, and my sister is siding with him." Ashton pushed Amora's hand away, sat up, and sent the stingy white hospital sheet into a raging avalanche that poured from his shoulders. His orbs bit coldly into the crisp gray of Charles's cores before he angrily grunted, "And the peasant still rules the day."

Along with a sharp glare, the senior's reply caught Ashton's tongue. "The peasant also protected the princess until he nearly bled to death, and your sister did not side with Alsyne. She merely told you to concentrate on yourself, which is wise advice from a lady of the Academy. I know we put Wing down because of his origins, but if you were there to witness what he did for Lukainy, you would come to the same conclusion that I have reached. McCallister is a knight…"

"I will crush him," Hunter spat after his body lurched forward. "I am not here for his amusement! I am a second-year student of the Academy with noble lineage, and I will not be held down by some trash picked out from the gutter."

"Alsyne is right," Charles retorted in a deep, lumbering voice. "It does not matter from where Wing came because in his heart there is a noble lurking. You have to come to grips with reality, Ashton; McCallister is Princess Lukainy's guardian whether you like it or not."

"In three days," Defy spoke into the slouching Ereint's ear, "the Hapsburg 7th Army will invade the Settlement of the Southern Tier under the banner of Cartheim. We are going back to war, my liege," he coaxed, "and you will once again lead Tistal against its sworn enemy by dispatching Wing to handle the situation alone." Derrick's voice became drenched in a serpentine tone as Conrad's raspy speech materialized for the first time in seven years. "And your little girl will finally become my bride. If you let her follow Wing, then I shall destroy her, your family, and your beloved kingdom. Do you understand King Ereint, or has age leeched your wisdom to the point that you will no longer adhere to my orders?"

"Lord Conrad," Ereint replied, his oculars appearing as darkened voids detached from the strong conscience that remained bound within his frail flesh. "Upon the first sighting of the 7th, I shall send Wing into your humble hands."

"Good, at least now Trigger is not here to take you away from your kind master."

"I am tired of you protecting me," Lukainy whispered into Wing's ear as she pulled the bed sheets up to her shoulders. He had his arms wrapped around her sweaty waist, and his eyes had grown wide from her words. "I want to fight with you," she said, "like we did at the end of the fight with Lara. I want us to be a team; I do not want to be on the sidelines any more, and I do not want you to act like you are my shield." Lightly, her fingers tapped his firm chest in a gentle rhythm that yearned to beat in time with Wing's heart.

"We will fight as one, Luky," her knight responded shyly, his irides enveloped by the twin overtones of care and concern. "I promise," he added, an additional affirmation sealed with a tender kiss that pressed his fangs against Luka's bottom lip.

Her hand ventured to his back with roaming fingertips that explored the space between his smooth skin and the damp sheet. "Stop talking," she ordered as her lips danced over Wing. Luky closed her eyes and shivered to the experience of his body sliding beneath her own. She felt the heat rise from him as if an inviting flame kindled atop her bed, and her mind yearned for the consummation that would come from being swept under her love. Creeks dripped down McCallister's legs as Marrok slid her knee to his side and gripped his waist. "And stop being shy," she continued as she guided her gentle warrior to his throne perched upon a princess.

The bloodstained sheet draped over Wing's head while his shocked stare pierced a wall of scruffy black hair to meet the white glimmer of Luka's enthralling grin. Her scherzando giggle drifted through the cadet's eardrum like a serenade for one of Shakespeare's star-crossed lovers, but the star-shaped scar drilled into his back made him push for a harmonious future that only the two of them could dare compose. The moist breath that brushed against her neck started the movement that descended towards her anxious curves, and snared to the beat was a soft grunt that perked Luky's ears from the firm base of the mattress. "Okay."

Her slender frame was crushed beneath Wing's dominating weight, and caring kisses prodded playful whimpers from their inner slumbers. "Why do you always have to protect me?" she spoke – a solo gripping the melody's reins. "Why do I have to be the damsel in distress?" Budding tears accompanied the waves of wind that rushed over her radiant flesh and kept her bound to Wing's intoxicating grip. "From now on," she whispered, her voice hushed by McCallister's delicacies, "I am going to be your knight."

Luka wondered if her incessant teasing had hidden this passionate side of Wing or if her obstinate nature had muted his whetting timbre and the ever-quickening tempo that brought the bourns of his maw to her skin. The rough bottoms of her feet dug into smooth silk, and a high-pitched moan shattered the temporary silence when her insides blossomed to his touch. "Then I'll play your prince."

She quivered to Wing's subdued response and quickly clutched his shoulders to drive him closer to the inferno pounding beneath her breasts. The tears of joy that welled in her canthi finally fled down her cheeks in trickles that joined her sweet music in freedom. "M-m-milord," she stuttered before Wing silenced her with a flavorful kiss laced with the forceful taste akin to that of melted chocolate.

Wing's eyes opened to reveal ochre cores that struck Luky's captive quintessence; his ears caught the rhythmic wails that broke from her lungs each time he descended to slide his dew dripping abs over her royal figure. The heat drew him closer, and Wing's thumbs could not resist stroking the blood red cheeks of the beautiful woman trapped by the loving embrace.

Wing felt the pull of Luky's claws on his shoulders, but he ignored her body's desperate attempts to escape the pleasure and pain that inundated her soul. Her psyche, however, gave a much different order. *Scream,* she thought. *Scream so that he knows you are his, scream until the pain is gone, and scream until the pleasure surrounds you!* Her fang sealed her lower lip in a last effort to contain the sexual howls that brewed in her bust. Yet, Wing's kiss set them free, and as her raging scream brought the piece to its perfect cadence, Wing drew back to an awaiting fermata and whispered, "You protect me more than you know."[5]

Jeanine, Harmony's voice bit into the queen's mind as she sat idly in her chamber of violet, *Conrad has made his move against Ereint.* "We cannot have your presence revealed, milady," the queen replied, glancing through the window pane at storm clouds clashing with a sky of blue. *Summon Kit and give him the parcel for Wing. The time of their great trial is at hand, and we must not interfere until the battle is over. However, we can discuss the renewed threat with King Adrian in Cartheim and hopefully avoid another war.*

"Will Adrian listen to you?" Jeanine asked in a secretive timbre after her eyes narrowed from a burst of lightning that cast its web across the heavens.

My brother gave him the throne, Harmony replied, *so he better listen to me.* She paused and allowed the fragments of her memory to seep into Jeanine's consciousness. A young boy's phrases rang throughout the cavern that comprised the queen's thoughts; a little red-haired, beaming-eyed child stood in the bombarded wasteland betwixt Tistal and Cartheim, stared into the amber eyes of his idol, and waited for Trigger's holy guidance. *He was always fond of that boy,* Harmony commented. *The two would spend hours upon hours training together; the real gift was the title of prince to Kit and not the title of king to Adrian -- although there was a special bond there too.*

"Queen Jeanine," Kit interrupted while his hand tapped the heavy wood door. "I have come as you requested."

Jeanine walked to her chestnut drawer and retrieved a large parcel from its zenith. "Come in Kit," she responded, turning to face the entryway as the officer appeared. "I would like you to give this package to Lukainy and have her present it to Wing." Kit froze and peered into her lenses; her request was simple enough, but the experienced knight could tell that something unseen was not right. The familiarity of her tone additionally embraced the recollections of his youth, but the exact setting eluded the captain's grasp. "Take care of Trigger," the queen spoke with piercing words that shot straight to his heart. "I am going to speak with your father, and whatever you do, do not approach Ereint alone."

"H-Ha…" he stuttered and stopped when the queen pressed her sacred hand against his trembling lips.

"This is merely a diplomatic mission, Prince Christopher; my presence will strictly be regarded as the visiting Queen Jeanine of Tistal."

She called me prince, Kit thought, shuddering from the word while his hand shook. "I understand, milady," he replied, linking the pieces of the puzzle. Ever since the day he witnessed Wing pull Daizer into the world, he knew that the boy housed Trigger's soul. An hour ago, Dai told him Lara's story about the return of Defy, and now, the elder sister of the twin kings stood before him behind the veil of Tistal's royal family.

The squeal of enamel grinding against enamel saturated Ashton's ears. He was still boiling mad, and his mind tinkered with the seeds of revenge when he halted in front of Wing's bedroom door. Deep shades of purple and black surrounded his left orb and covered his cheek, but the sight of such wounds paled in comparison to the pain gripping the boy's nerves. He knew that he could not do anything too serious or the princess would have a field day with him, but he had to strike back at Wing's honor as well as Derrick's pride; he had to redeem himself. "I will beat McCallister," he growled. Anxious and angered scribbles infected the parchment through which the silver tip of a dagger struck. Splints of wood fell to the floor, and the paper caught the breeze drifting from Ashton's bulging arm before it rested lightly against the worn maple slab.

"I am still keeping my eye on you, Hunter," Charles spoke. His words added a gentler two-part harmony to the air that dampened Ashton's maniacal solo, and his hands pulled back locks of deep-brown hair to reveal his soothing stare. "After today, we cannot look at Wing in the manner we have in the past. He was beaten to near death in a sparring match and took more hits for Lukainy than any commissioned knight has in a lifetime. That Lara von Alsyne is amazing; my imagination cannot fathom the pain her strokes brought to him, but Wing still pulled off a victory."

"It is like you said, Charles; I was not there!" Specs of white foam sparkled under the glare of candlelight tongues that reached from stone-tied posts. "I do not give a damn about what he did in front of you! In front of me, he is a poor boy that needs to be put back in his place; in front of me, he is a fraud and a cheat that has yet to prove anything except that he is a victor by fluke! He does not win because of his skill; he wins because he carries around a Marrok."

"You are out of…"

"Save it for someone who cares, Chuck." Wing's presence illuminated the darkened corridor, and the taps of his leather boots against the damp rock accompanied the crescents of amber that rose over his irides. "You're acting like a dog, Ashton. Look at yourself! You're slobbering throughout the hallway like a madman with abandon. Do you still not trust me, or are you acting like a baby because you can't stand that Luky chose me over you?" Wing glanced at the note stapled to his door and smirked. "I'll accept your challenge, Ashton, and then I'll take pride in beating into your skull that the history I have with Luky transcends your petty bullshit."

"Wing, as the senior classman, I cannot condone…"

"I know Charles," Wing interrupted again and stepped up to Ashton. "You don't think I have skill, Hunter? Maybe you missed the memo that said skill doesn't come attached with over-inflated and pompous chivalric values; it comes from the love you have for your comrades and countrymen. Do you even believe or follow the shit you preach? Do you really go out of your way to protect those who aren't loaded like your family, or do you shaft them all like you shaft me?"

"Shut your damn mouth!" Ashton retorted before he pushed Wing back. "Get the fuck outside and show me your supposed brilliance!"

Wing cracked his knuckles and examined Ashton's burning panes. "Well, that's not very noble of you, is it?" he countered. "If you're willing to come out from behind your hereditary cloak and your knife's shroud, then I'll show you that I'm not just an undeserving poor boy."

Lightning lit up the darkened sky, and thunder rumbled as the trio emerged into the courtyard. Charles took his position under the archways, deciding to stay sheltered from the rain that drenched the faces of Ashton and Wing. The soggy mess of grass and mud coiled around their boots with every step, and competition's spark flashed betwixt every harsh gaze. "Are you ready?" Ashton snarled and dug his toe into the slop as a raindrop gripped one of his bangs.

Charles's eyebrows sank when he peered over the field. *They really are going to go through with it then,* he thought, a sigh passing through his lips. *Kit could punish them severely for this, but I guess it cannot be helped.*

"Did you even need to ask?" Wing replied. Stoked by his undying passion for Luky, and untouched by the rain that raked his skin, the fire in his eyes refused to be extinguished. Once more, thunder's pride captivated the heavens with its tiger roar while Wing dug the ball of his foot into the mire and pushed forward. Droplets froze like winter crystals suspended on time's razor wire in the infinite, adagio expanse that bound the hearts of two competitors. However, faced with the wills of leather, hide, and knuckle, that boundless domain shattered into shards of glass fearful of each determined step and every flung fist.

Book 1 – Episode 5

Power chords of lightning, cymbal crashes of thunder, and lyrics forced into existence by pounding fists painted the grim courtyard picture. Provoked by rattling anger, clumps of soggy sludge flew from the heels of the cadets' boots and rolled across the snare formed by the thin film of water that covered the ground. Through one eye, Wing looked at his opponent, for the other was covered in a veil of blood that poured from his cut brow. However, the burning ochre that coated the visible iris spoke one sentence loud and clear; *don't tread on me.*[6]

Ashton charged and fired a punch with his right hand that Wing easily blocked. While the knight had landed a few hard blows with his crimson-coated knuckles, his oculars had become tainted with a reply to Wing's brewing flames. *Settle the score,* he thought, rolling his knee into Wing's gut as a fist cracked his jaw.

Waves of mud splattered against exposed teeth when both fell to the ground and panted for air. Lines of red mixed with dirty brown, and amber caught hazel in a fierce gaze that pulled the men back to their feet. With his hand gripping his chest, Wing spoke, "Not bad."

"Not bad yourself," Ashton replied, hurling a glob of maroon spit from the confines of his mouth. The music paused, silenced by an ascending transposition that sharpened the words en route to the coming *but.* "But you are still an unwanted peasant."

In the meantime, Wing found his base and pushed his foot through inches of a tainted triad composed of fallen grass, reddish gobs, and black mush. His cheeks were scarred with a crisscross of crusted scratches that whiskered his face in a tiger-like mesh. The roar of kin rumbled in the sky above, the tongues of lightning reflected off the corners of his eyes, and the wind of nature fueled his claw-baring strike against Ashton's battered body.

Inside, Kit stood at attention upon the threshold of Lukainy's chamber. He stared at the princess who had immediately torn Harmony's package to shreds and analyzed the black and ochre armor that clung to the divine wind of the Battle Flame. *He will awaken,* Kit pondered, unable to ignore the faded images of his childhood idol. "Make sure Wing receives those," he spoke, only to be immediately hushed by Luka's waving hand.

She admired the pattern sewn into the cloak of the leather piece: a white tiger constructed of dichromatic sheets that burst from the hide like embers rising from a mighty inferno. "Truly amazing," she commented quietly before her confused gray orbs sought answers from the knowledge tied to Kit's past. "Christopher," she spoke with a sharpening tone and an emerging scowl, "why is Wing receiving a noble's armor?"

The captain tapped his foot and sighed, for his princely duties and disaster seemed to always pair in a cacophonous duet that grated his mind. *If I tell her, then she will be worried and will want the whole story, but if I keep it a secret and she discovers the truth…*

"Christopher…" Luka's words soaked his thoughts in a drowning layer of hallucinated sound. Her eyes crushed the void with demonic beams of red as a noose-wielding hand brushed aside the sea of darkness. "You never told me that – as Trigger's vessel – Wing held the lineage to Cartheim's crown, and you never told me about the danger that came attached to that legacy. I'm going to kill you, Kit…"

"Kit!" the princess wailed, snapping the soldier back from the realm of his overactive imagination. "Are you going to give me an answer, or do you not have one to give?"

He replied with a hefty sigh, "Those robes belonged to Trigger. Unfortunately milady, I do not have much else to tell you, but I can say that Wing will need you at his side more than he ever has."

"That's not a very descriptive answer…"

"He wandered off," Amora growled, searching the castle halls for a vengeful brother. "Wing may be Lukainy's pet, but there is no reason for Ashton to pick a fight with him." She bit her lip and huffed through her nose when a clear yelp rang through the corridor. "Combat outside of training sessions is explicitly forbidden!"

Upstairs, Luky and Kit heard the yelp as well, and they immediately ran to the window. "Idiot!" Marrok shouted, dropping Trigger's armor while her sight affixed to the boys' jabs and strikes. Her knuckles turned white as her fingers clenched the windowsill, and with a rising rage, she shoved Kit aside and stomped down the stairwell. Shining locks of deep brown and the scent of citrus perfume caught Luka's attention throughout her descent, and a moment later, two stubborn women stood face-to-face in a passageway much too small to contain the brewing emotion. "Amora! What the hell is your brother doing with Wing? Is calling him names not enough to satisfy your family's arrogance?"

Amora sneered and started marching with Lukainy towards the courtyard doors. "As if," she pouted, digging her polished nails deeply into the skin of her palms. "I admit that calling Wing names was wrong. Derrick and Charles are right, but you cannot blame my family for its strict adherence to the rules of our class."

"I chose him to be my knight!" Lukainy yelled. "That alone should be enough to justify his presence."

"Why?" she retorted, cocking her head back to reveal wolfish fangs. "Is it only because he saved your life when you were ten? Wing was a thief, Luka, and you were once my best friend! How could he possibly know what it's like to be a noble?"

The princess scowled and snarled. "And you would still be my friend if you gave him a chance!" The bulky gate drew closer at a quickening pace as the riff the two girls played grew more boisterous with every drum tap and each accented word that followed their strides.

"Well, maybe I am trying now!" Amora cried before the pair planted their boots against the doors and kicked them open.

Charles jolted from his post when the girls appeared and squinted at the dissonant shriek of the knights' names that shook the school grounds. Ashton and Wing froze, their orbs slowly moving to face the cloud of mire and dust that rapidly approached. Their nerves quickly tingled from the painful grips on their ears, and their hearts beat in fear from the piercing glares that crushed their prides. "I told you not to get hurt!" Luky screamed, pulling the bloodied Wing to the grand stone archways.

"And I told you to get your rest and focus on getting better!" Amora interjected, tugging Ashton to a spot on the grass to tend to his wounds.

"Expelling them is out of the question," Kit whispered, his gentle knock pulling Dai from his quarters. The captain held Wing's sword to his tan hide armor along with two bags containing Trigger's garments and battle supplies owned by Amora, Ashton, and Lukainy. "The four of them will just have to learn to work together on the field," he mumbled upon emerging into the pouring rain.

Kit's ears perked to the conversations that transpired on opposite sides of the yard. "If I didn't love you, I'd beat the shit out of you for disobeying me," Luky growled in Wing's ear while a hand slapped his scab-covered cheek. "You are better than that Wing, and I expected better from you."

"Ashton Hunter," Amora blared, "I do not care how upset you are over Wing's appointment. Fighting a peasant over such a petty squabble is a disgrace to the family, and – so help me Aurora – you are going to find a way to repent for your actions."

Kit's wine-red eyes swept the field once more after he coughed, stepped onto the grass, and set the bags down carefully. "The four of you have had some serious problems," he began, "and you need to know that I have grown tired of them. You have shown tremendous growth, but an outburst like this one could have made it to the headmaster. Do not turn progress into rubbish. With that said, consider yourselves lucky that I am going to be the one to give the punishment.

"To start, all of you will walk 25 klicks to the west to investigate and eliminate a group of bandits that have been terrorizing the town of Hemarn. The only information the palace has received is that the group consists of a dozen men; accounts regarding the bandits' weapon and transportation preferences were inconsistent."

"Are you serious, Kit?" Marrok replied. Her irides burned with anger and she beamed menacing scowls towards Wing and Ashton. "You want Amora and I punished for their transgressions?"

No, Kit thought, rubbing his tensed brow with his thumb and index finger. *I just do not want Wing and Ashton to kill one another.* "You two are just as much at fault," he lied. "Princess, you are the one saying that you do not want Wing to fight alone; thus, I have given you the chance to fight by his side. Regardless of whether you appreciate my reasoning or not, a member of the medical squad should always accompany a knight anyway, and I see two volunteers sitting in the rain with two very troublesome boys.

"Enough bickering," he continued, retrieving one of the bags during his first step towards Amora and Ashton. "Lady Hunter, I collected your potions, bandage supplies, and miscellaneous ointments. Ashton, your two combat daggers are in this bag as well. These contents are all you shall receive for this mission; take care of your garments because the replacements are commoner issues."

Wing sighed and wiped some water from Luky's dampened cheek; the rain had finally stopped, but the sky tears that soaked the five caught in the storm failed to cleanse the emotional dirt that soiled their souls. Luka pouted and closed her eyes, refusing to make contact with the one she loved. *Ridiculous,* she thought as worry and sorrow wove two strings that bound her heart.

"Please forgive me," Wing spoke in her ear before he stood to greet Kit. The royal did not acknowledge his request, but the bitter cold she felt when he pulled away left her devastated. Kit was right; she did not want him to fight alone any more, but her stubborn mind had already chosen the path that would force Wing to re-earn her graces.

"Lukainy," Kit coughed, "I have included your medical kit and whip in this sack. Wing, there is a new suit of armor in here for you that I would like you to wear now; it is a gift from the princess and her mother." His lips spread into a sly grin fueled by the memories of Trigger, Lutti, and the armor that drove her mad with passion. *Hopefully, this will bring a smile to your face, Lukainy,* Kit thought, watching as Wing departed for the doors with a wad of black leather in his crimson-stained hands.

Wing's cheeks turned a deep red when he placed the outfit atop his straw mattress. "Is this really armor?" he asked, running his fingertips over the garments that failed to resemble anything that he had ever worn in training. As if he were being watched, Wing shyly stripped, his heart pounding heavier with every second that passed. Slowly, he slid the jock strap up his legs and felt the hide settle into his skin while an internal ember lit the fuse of his second psyche. He gulped, grabbed the pair of chaps, and snapped them around his legs and waist. The warmth within continued to build until the amber streaks that were ever-present in his soft brown irides burned with a brightness not seen by his generation. Next, came the belted boots that slid over his dark socks; the soles were thick and tough – the authority of the ensemble – as if they were formed to shatter the rocks over which they traveled.

The vest doesn't even protect the shoulder blades, Wing realized, but for some reason, he did not mind when he slid it over his torso. Despite the openness of the armor, the knight felt feverish heat seep from his flesh and noticed the sweat that dripped from every pore when he finally took hold of the byakko-embroidered cape. By the time he let the cloak fall to his back, and by the time he had the string around his neck tightly tied, Wing panted from the blaze that surged through his heart.

His tongue brushed against the feline-like fangs that his teeth had become, and his oculars looked at arms that gleamed under the flicker of his window candle. *Get going,* a voice barked, and with a single breath, the room plunged into darkness.

Outside, the feel of blistering warmth captivated Lukainy's senses; her ears perked to Wing's stride, her nose detected his slightly changed scent, and her fingers flexed anxiously for something to touch. *He's different,* she thought, waiting for him to emerge from the castle while an equally stubborn feminine tone wrapped itself around a mind's ear. It waited in silence until the doors submitted to Wing's hands, until the princess found her knight with love-struck eyes, and until she finally bolted towards the thrill of his embrace. *My king is coming home*, it spoke; *my king is coming home.*[7]

Book 1 – Episode 6

Kit twitched when his chestnut eyes set the shimmering Lara in their sights. Her characteristic straps loosened when she pressed into the captain, and her lips lurched forward as she sculpted a tempting pout. "What do you mean, Kit?" she asked, tightening her grip. Her voice spiraled into a soft, yet menacing growl. "You sent them on a mission at the worst possible time."

The officer slid back into the wall, attempting to gain some distance and answer the question clawing his brain. *How does Dai deal with her?* "I had to punish them for their recklessness," he responded. "Ashton and Wing need to learn to get along if they want to earn their places in the Elite Guard, and Amora and Luky need to be present to keep the boys under control. I did not have much of a choice; if I did not punish them, then they could have been expelled."

"I needed to speak to Marrok," she snarled in his ear. "Dai told me to come see her, and now, I won't have the chance until she returns. Conrad has made his move, which means that we all must be on our toes." She brushed his scruff with her nails and smirked at the shiver that worked its way down to his feet. The blade's fingers crawled to his cheek to deliver a light push before she sauntered away. "Don't flatter yourself, Kit; I only want metal as my sex toy."

A crescent moon peered from behind the veil of a twilight sky at the foursome walking down the deserted white gravel road to Hemarn. The air remained tainted by tension as if the free breeze that combed the heroes' strands of hair was a labyrinth of lead bricks poisoning them with every step. "W-Wing," Amora stuttered, attempting to break the invisible wall that divided the party. "How are you feeling?"

"I'm alright," he replied after Dai's secret words of advice nipped his psyche's ear. His byakko cape fluttered in the wind when he turned his head to face Luky, and a grin stretched the corners of his lips. With an accompanying tap to one of the bandages taped to his cheek, he continued, "The princess is an excellent medic."

"Idiot," Ashton retorted, his stride having carried him far ahead of the pack. "Of course Lukainy is an excellent medic! She should not be wasting her time taking care of a damn slave." He stopped and spun around, pointing to the tattoo sewed onto Wing's hand. "You wear the truth, McCallister!"

"Ashton, what is wrong with you?" Amora wailed before crisp sea hues met her brother's stunned hazel orbs. "You are my blood and my closest companion, but this squabbling with Wing is getting old.

You two had your fight and look at where it got us: twenty kilometers from the palace with no roof over our heads."

A smile blossomed and eradicated the stern countenance that had bound Luka's face; maybe Amora was trying to mend the rift that had grown between them over the years, but – despite Dai's consultation – Wing remained skeptical. "Didn't you call me filthy just a day ago?" he asked, his boots digging into the ground when he came to a halt.

Ashton took a step forward, groomed his hair, and formed a fist. "Do not talk to my sister in that manner, peasant!" he began, only to be hushed when the princess wrapped her arms around Wing's waist.

"That's enough," Luky spoke into his ear. "You two are on the same side, and Amora is only trying to improve our situation."

Wing tenderly caressed the soft skin that gripped his leather vest, and he glanced at the reconciler. "Is that what you want?" he asked her while his thumb stroked his partner's knuckle. McCallister smiled in response to Amora's reassuring nod, and he looked towards Ashton with a firm glare pricked by an olive-branch sparkle.

With a sigh breaching his lips, Hunter continued his trek down the road. "I'm not your best friend now, and I will still prove that I am the better knight; however, a truce is fine with me if it is what they want."

He could not think what he wished or speak what his tongue desired, but Derrick told the banished tale with his slouching structure and sagging expression. His oculars, which once emitted passion and mystique, appeared dull through the lens of Lara's scrutiny; and his rhythm, which once fervently pounded to repel the blues, seemed faint compared to Dai's melody.

There they stood, face-to-face, in Alsyne's sanctuary, where the light leaked by stars passed through tinted windowpanes to prod the choir from its sandman slumber. "Are you ready for the battle to come?" Derrick finally asked, but the phrases flowing from his curled fingers spoke a different question.

I can tell that this is hard on you, Lara determined as concern's anxious beat threaded its strings into the cavity that once housed her jewel. However, she could not comfort her sweet master, for hidden beneath his gentle nature stood a cave of doubt that housed a wretched leech. With one word, the bloodsucking beast could emerge, doused in the dripping filth of his sins, to extinguish Defy's flame with the snap of a finger. Through this crippling mine, where the stench of decomposing bodies, the stains of war, and the lingering fear of the collapse remained at the forefront of one's anamneses, Lara crawled for Defy's sake. "I'll protect you as I always do."

Ashton's narrowed sight fell upon the prairie grasses that grew off the trodden path. "You mean we have to sleep here?" he asked, cringing at the prospect, for he already knew the answer that Wing had made abhorrently clear. "I know!" he groaned after gazing at his rival. "We cannot risk being seen by the bandits until we have done enough reconnaissance."

"It's not that bad, Hunter," McCallister replied apathetically. He did not care about Ashton's ridiculous insecurities; he was entranced by the siren's glow that reflected off Lukainy's robes and skin from the rays of the sky's snow-powder arch. The flakes that fell to Wing's triggered essence melted into a torrent that energized Luka's unique blue aura.

He stood silently and swore that he saw ocean locks drift across her brow. But such illusions were merely time's tricks targeting a trapped soul with subtle reminders for a love once held. "Lutti," Wing whispered as the heat rekindled beneath his armor.

I know he's watching me, Marrok thought before she turned. Even without looking into his loving eyes, she felt the warmth that accompanied his ochre-laced affection, inhaled his pure scent that saturated the dew-soaked atmosphere, and promoted amorous aspirations that became her imagination's reality. She shifted her gaze and peered through delusion's lens at the sable semblance shooting from Wing's pores, and – captivated – Luky marched forth.

Her hands rose from her sides and sought to reach through those dreamt flames to an imprisoning hug. Everything yielded to the moonlight mist, the suspension through which she had to fight, but eventually, Luka touched his torso and succumbed to the chimeral visions that murmured Trigger to her ears.

"Hey there," Wing said. His lips curled into a sheepish smile before his thumbs ventured to cradle her cheeks. *She's exhausted,* he figured, guiding her head to rest against the base of his neck. "It looks like I get to take care of you tonight." Shyly, Wing dropped to his knees, all the while supporting her with a firm grasp that kept her speechless. The cold air nipped at the exposed flesh between his jockstrap and chaps until the knight drew his princess close to press his lips to her ear. "I'll be your mattress."

Lukainy jolted when cherry blossoms bloomed beneath her orbs, and her mind fell victim to the onslaught of embarrassment that overwhelmed her thoughts. She wanted to slap him but stopped as the palm of her hand cupped the bandages covering his face. "You are going too fast," she whispered prior to sealing a kiss that forced him to the ground. "Why do you do this to me?" she proceeded, sliding her arms underneath his vest.

Buried beneath sheets of leather, bent grasses strove skyward, pushing into the sparking flames of battle and health that rested atop their domains. Nature hushed itself, wishing to play the part of an enthralled audience that watched one of its more benevolent acts transpire upon a stage mostly constructed in war. "It's because I can," Wing asserted as he raked the small of her back and blanketed the duo with her cloak.

"Idiot," Luka replied, putting her hands on his shoulders, "that will just make me retaliate." She grinned, stared into his eyes, and moved closer until the tip of her nose brushed against his face. His redolence grew stronger with every breath that became trapped between his leather and her cloth. As she bit his lower lip, Lukainy hoped that he was feeling and noticing the same thing that she did: their hearts were beating as one.

"W-what are they doing?" Ashton gagged while gawking at the lump beneath the princess's robes.

"They are sleeping!" Amora swiftly kicked her brother in the back of the knee and watched him tumble to the ground with a shocked yelp. "And you should do the same."

The slow tapping of steps echoed throughout the void corridor, where light from neither sun nor moon peered through windows of stone to devour the musty odor that filled the air. Suddenly, a pair of snake eyes emerged from the darkness to illuminate the path under the order of a sinister green flame. "I see that you have arrived, Wolfe."

"Lord Conrad," a woman barked, stepping forward to bathe in the scattering beam that leaked from his oculars. Except for the blood-colored annuli and a canine grin that glistened in harmony with her kin's greed-driven fire, her features remained covered by the veil of night. "The Hapsburg 7th is reporting as ordered. Do you have any idea how much it took for me to get the other six members to come?" Wolfe snapped. "This mission of yours better be..."

"I want you to kill the boy," he interrupted. "One of my attendants prepared Cartheim armor for each of you. Go stir up trouble in the Southern Tier until McCallister comes to the rescue. I told Defy that you would wait three days before the advance, but if they become restless, then feel free to go as soon as you wish. And Rachael," he added, "you can toy with the brat all you want, but make sure that he dies. While Tistal and Cartheim plummet into a chaos that embraces the coming of a second war, I will take the woman forever meant to be my bride."

A thin layer of sweat coated Luky's cheeks when she awoke. Her rendezvous with Wing beneath the cloak grew hot under the azure heavens, and every sniff she took absorbed the sweet aroma of his fondled form. "Wake up," she purred in his ear before her teeth grazed his neck. "If you take too long, then I will have to teach you a lesson." Another breath avalanched into her lungs and she slyly wrapped her hands around his waist.

After a groan escaped his throat and a wrist stroked his brow, Wing revealed the brown irides that Luka yearned to see. "Hey," he said groggily, trying to focus his sight in their weakly lit paradise. Yet his efforts were soon for naught when a giggle's breeze pulled the princess's cloak high into the air. Wing squinted – caught off-guard by the blazing rays of the sun – and froze to the wet texture of her buss driving into his lips. "Mmf," he huffed, struggling from the tightening grip that held both sides of his jockstrap.

A smear of red and orange hues painted the biological canvas that blindfolded Wing, a succulent shade of pink coated the pair of locks that held his tongue in check, and the smell of blueberries filled his nostrils with a forced gasp that pulled Luky to the most sacred ecstasy of McCallister's dreams. He was drowning in her affection, hallucinating vivid images that placed them in fields of flowers on a sunny day, and craving her complete touch.

He squirmed and tried to retain a sliver of his captured pride, but his master merely held her kiss until the pulsing pant against her cheek dwindled into a submissive wind that begged for more. At that moment, Luka began her retreat and hovered above his attractive physique with Wing's lower lip still bound. McCallister's head rolled back and he prayed that she would not let the passion end right when he gave in to her assault. His ears perked, attentive to their beloved's words, and quietly Wing awaited the outcome. "Good luck on your mission, cadet," she cooed upon completing her exit. "But do not fret for you will taste the rest when you bring honor to your princess."

Why has he summoned me? Kit thought upon entering Ereint's throne room. The chamber was darker than usual as if the menacing storm clouds that had rolled through the previous day infiltrated the castle and clung to the rugged stone. "You called for me, Your Majesty?"

"I heard that you know the whereabouts of McCallister and my daughter," the king began with a raspy voice. Its kindness had been replaced by a coarse layer of deceit that chilled Christopher's core.

"I sent the Hunters, Wing, and Lukainy on a mission as punishment for fighting outside of scheduled training, my liege," Kit replied while his maroon eyes busily studied the sovereign. The captain could not possibly mistake the aura that coated Ereint's wandering soul. It made his body shudder the same way it had during the Great War, made his mind think of Trigger's hate-filled growl, and left him with only one name.

"I already know that piece of information," Ereint responded. "I just want to know where you sent them."

I should not be telling him anything if he's already fallen into Conrad's control, but I cannot risk it. "Hemarn, sir," he continued. "They are taking the bandit case that we received and will probably return in a day or two." Kit noticed the emerald haze that clouded the ruler's irides and stopped.

"I have decided that as your special candidate," Ereint explained while shifting his mass towards the front of his chair, "Wing needs to display a greater level of maturity than the other students. Therefore, upon his arrival, I will give a special assignment for him to complete alone. I expect you to outfit a supply pack, at once."

"As you wish, King Ereint." He hesitated, wondering if the real royal was waiting somewhere beneath Conrad's shell. He bowed and stared at the cracks in floor as his brain computed the possible outcomes and consequences. *I have to try*, he concluded, lifting his head before speaking, "Is there anything else you would like me to do?"

The monarch sighed and paused while his hands trembled atop elegantly carved armrests, and his lips quivered ahead of the sentence that wished to escape Conrad's mind-numbing clutch. The tongues of fire that surrounded the king's pupils faded and struggling pants guided his wind to freedom. The soothing baritone Kit heard became crystal-clear as though a lake clouded by sand suddenly settled into a state of unaltered azure purity. "Her happiness," he said before his back rested against the throne's cushion. "Her happiness…"

Book 1 – Episode 7

The bright morning that had greeted the foursome eventually faded into an overcast sky with colors and shades that matched the stone orbs of Princess Lukainy. "Why are we crawling through the brush when we could just walk down the road?" Ashton whispered in Wing's ear.

"For a noble, you have a pretty poor set of tactical skills," Wing replied with a sigh. "Nature is giving us free camouflage, and it would be foolish for us to shrug it off and walk into a potential trap. This area is supposedly the primary raid route of the bandits that we are supposed to find, but…"

"We should find them on our own terms," Hunter interrupted with a witty tone on his tongue and a smug grin on his lips that led McCallister to believe that perhaps his arrogant colleague possessed as much bite as he did bark.

"And if we still want to do that," Lukainy interrupted, pressing the two boys' heads into the prairie grasses with smooth strokes of her forearms, "then we should remind ourselves of the definition of stealth."

Amora crouched behind the trio and turned her ear to the wind upon which the strained melody of a child's voice played. "There's trouble down the road," she murmured matter-of-factly before her stare captured the gaze of the princess.

In the meantime, Wing had pressed his body to the dirt. Blades of grass nipped at his exposed skin, and the earth parted to welcome tense fingers that sought shelter from distraction. "There are fourteen pairs of unique human footsteps," he informed while continually feeling the subtle drumming that surfed the plains, "four horses, and a wagon."

Twelve robes of white hung like ghostly sheets over concealed pillars of flesh and bone. No sound came from the roaming spirits of torture aside from the hideous scraping of steel against rock and the crackling pops that burst when spear-point separated the body from its essence. No remorse seeped through the veil that shrouded the attacker as it watched a small child cling to her blood-soaked father. The spear retreated and left behind a shattered spine and a nearly decapitated protector whose remains became enshrined by the relatively small hands of a green-eyed brunette.

Much like her aggressors, the girl produced no noise; neither screams nor cries shattered the solemn seal of tears that fell to the earth or stained her tattered earthen-colored clothes. What could she do? Fingernails found palm as the pressure to act compressed her fists into tight balls, but her father was the provider and the guardian. There was no one else that could save the fruits of labor from the greedy hands of murderous outlaws. She watched, horrified, as the one that killed her dad directed the others to cut the horses free and pillage the rest.

Un-victimized by the anger that consumed the child's heart, the loyal steeds that had served the family fled. From deep within, love boiled and coated the soul with a crust of hatred that hardened with every passing moment, and the girl's pulse quickened when the spike of adrenaline finally crested atop the wave of chaos. She lunged towards the crimson-bathed argent tip and yearned to sever the ties that bound the robber to the world of the living, but all she found were the shades of night and the faint, fleeting scent of man.

Wing held the kid in his arms and gazed – while tongues of ochre licked his irides – at the blood pouring from her chest. The bandit's spear had claimed another innocent life, yet the raw emotion from that girl's soul lingered as fuel for dormant flames. Idolizing youths surged throughout the playground of Wing's psyche and coaxed his disgust. "Killing a child," he bit with a demonic fervor, "is absolutely disgraceful."[8]

No time was wasted between Wing's statement and the first scrape of the spear-blade against Dai's skin. *There is something odd about that weapon,* he promptly informed the knight before using another contact to collect additional data. *Keep your distance, Wing. I am pretty sure these guys are using toxins.*

"Cheap bastards," McCallister grunted while his resentment continued to grow. "Using poison on your weapons too. I won't forgive you for what you have done!" Dirt and gravel parted beneath the sole when Wing lunged forward, and his razor – like a ray sent from the sun – cut through the fog. His shoulder plowed into the thug and drove the aggressor to the ground as the others launched their attacks. With agile turns, Wing evaded every strike and slipped unscathed into an internal mirage that surrendered the judge's gavel.

"Something is wrong," Luky spoke to Amora and Ashton. Minutes earlier, the paladin had remained in a calm, methodical state that produced rational decisions and sound tactical calculations; in the sparks of this battle, however, a bipolar shift blew Wing to the tundra of recklessness. To the princess, it was as though she stared at a completely different person.

"What the hell are you doing?" Ashton grumbled, running to Wing's aid with his silver daggers twirling about his fingers. "What happened to intelligence gathering and stealth? Or are you just turning into a fucking hypo…"

Wing pointed his sword towards the dead girl and retorted, "That." The somber, husky tone rolled over the earth like a tiger waiting to pounce and immediately hushed the taken aback Hunter.

The teen brushed his blond hair with one of his daggers and smirked. Regardless of Wing's thoughts or feelings, they were in a fight and had to uphold the honor of the kingdom. "The girl does not concern us. This group fits the profile given to us by Kit, which means that we have likely found our mission objective."

McCallister dwelled upon Ashton's rhetoric and he loathed it. The scent of blood that clung to the dissipating fog accompanied the thousands of wartime snapshots that ventured from the anamnestic abyss. He could hear another voice inside him crying to vivid scenes of rotting corpses and could picture wailing children clinging to maggot infested gore that had once made a soldier; he could feel that other heart burn its way towards the surface, and that raw emotional fire pushed him past the brink of insanity and into the pack of bandits. His renegade fang hacked at steel and wood in the vengeful pursuit of retribution on behalf of those whom the outlaws had killed.

The thieves refused to break their silence or the bond that held them in battle. Quickly they moved, each a snowflake in a blizzard that precipitated from the desperate mist. Their spears, daggers, and swords pointed towards the pair of knights who quickly found themselves surrounded by the group of mysterious attackers. "The blades are poisoned, Ashton," Wing mentioned before the screech of grating steel pierced his eardrums.

Meanwhile, Luky stood on the sidelines and bit her bottom lip with her canine tooth. The shift in Wing's attitude scared her; he had never displayed a passion to vengefully kill another person, but her own second soul hinted that such behavior was not uncommon in decades past. His wild battle cries nipped her ears as the grays of her eyes drifted to follow every darting movement that McCallister made. Like a musician deranged by the shrieks of his own instrument, Wing sliced through his enemies with every frantic stroke. His twisted combat genius smeared dark hues of red across the fabrics of white that covered the unforgiving ground in the perfect canvas.

Amora's crisp blue oculars observed the scene thoroughly. *Wing has taken out four; Ashton has taken out two,* she thought, peering at the weapons. "I need one for research," she informed Luky quietly and took a step towards the fallen bandits.

Marrok's eyes remained affixed to the sweat beading atop Wing's skin. Her hand clenched the handle of her whip as fear sunk its claws into her tender heart. The wails and taunts that dripped from Wing's mouth cast Amora's comments to deafened ears and froze Luka to the core. Yet the dread that accompanied Wing's rage paled in comparison to the thought of her knight fighting alone; thus, with a defrosting scream, the princess let her whip fly.

Yards away, Ashton jumped and imbedded one of his daggers into the skull of his opponent. Shouting, the plebe drove the dead bandit into the dirt with his knee and retrieved his weapon as a wry grin took control of his face. With every kill, he brought more glory to his kingdom, and with every second he lived, Ashton brought more honor to himself.

McCallister's fiery orbs saw past the two enemies that stood in his way and ignored the third caught by Luky's whip. His distraught conscience retained the hatred for the one who killed the child, commanded the group of dishonorable scum, and set sights upon Ashton Hunter. "Get out of my way," he roared and charged forward.

Luka lowered her center of mass and stared at the looter that dashed towards her. The slack whip still hung around the brigand's neck when calm advice guided Marrok. *Evade to the right, push off the ground, and plant your fist into the gut.* The glimmer of a spear passed to the left side of Luky's head as she ducked. Years of overprotection eroded beneath the torrent that forced one of Lukainy's fists into her adversary's abdomen and compelled the other to slam its knuckles into the delinquent's jaw.

"Nice knockout, milady," Amora said after her fingers wrapped around the lance of Luky's prey. "You spared me a trip."

Lightning struck twice when Dai's blade separated two heads from their necks. Every step brought Wing closer to the brink, his soul ached from the heat of the fight, and his mind refused to shake the image of the little girl that died in his arms. "Too fucking slow," he yelled, stepping behind the still-crouched Ashton to block the advance of the pack-leader.

"You're dead," the crook spoke – a woman whose tone had been saturated by lust and greed. Wing winced and peered at the blood seeping from his bicep.

Ashton stood and surveyed the cherry creek that poured from his rival and partner. "What are you doing?" he shouted, pulling Wing to his side before noticing the burning orange that consumed McCallister's irides.

"The chance of his death is zero," Amora interrupted. She held a vial of green liquid in her hand and smirked at the bandit. "The hallucinogenic addition is meaningless; snake venom derivatives can be counteracted by a proper mix of potions five and nine."

"It won't matter if I kill you and destroy your antidote," the woman replied and targeted the medic.

Wing put his hand on Ashton's shoulder for support and sneered. Within his mind, a voice rambled; its bickering with reason was infuriating, and every word and tormenting memory that trickled into his consciousness fed the flames only death could alleviate. "Get away," he ordered Hunter upon shoving Dai into the teen's hands. The hero's heart grew weak from the poison; however, his spirit grew stronger. Wing's knuckles burned as revulsion birthed fists. The opportunity to turn back had been ignored and McCallister lunged forward with all of his might.

The others stood beside the inferno that erupted from the cadet's body and were captivated by the five runic letters that seared his flesh. Orange flames burst from the warrior's fingers as he lodged them into the bandit's neck to dig through muscle and tissue with the hopes of finding her spine. They shifted through the meat while the woman twitched – held bound by the tightening grip – and locked around vertebrae that crumbled from the pressure.

Wing's voice would not be the last the outlaw heard. While poisoned blood bubbled from McCallister's mouth, a howling stranger roared, "Only the guilty will die when I am king." Finally, rage snapped and pulled the trigger. Brown, crusted clumps of skin peeled from the woman as she was devoured by an amber blaze. Clots of boiling bodily fluids that sought escape ruptured muscles and sent pieces of gore hurling into the air. Fire seemed to flow like rivers down legs that shook uncontrollably, and globs of melted muscle dripped from masterless limbs. Organs uncoiled and exploded from the charring mass as Wing carried the roasting corpse down the road in a death march that ended with bones submitting embers to the wind. His coughing increased as he threw the remaining ashes to the sky and gazed upon the letters that evaporated back into the mist from whence they came.

ᛏᚱᛁᚷᚱ

"It can't be," Ashton muttered while Amora rushed to the fallen Wing. However, Hunter saw it with his own two eyes and those letters were unmistakable. "Who is he, really?" he whispered, still clenching Dai by the hilt.

"Stop standing around, you two!" Amora called to Ashton and Luky. *They let a peasant into the Academy, and now we all know why, Trigger.* She poured the antidote into Wing's mouth and smiled as Marrok knelt by her side to lift the patient's head. "He will be fine, Your Highness," she continued. "Considering his identity, I do not think we have much to fear."

"Losing him," Luka replied softly. Tears welled and her fingers pressed firmly into his skin. "Is that the pain that dwells within us?" she asked. "It's a curse that has infected us all along."

"Or a gift," Dai's tone chimed in her ear after his human form appeared to the trio.

Ashton pointed at the soul-forge with a trembling, emptied hand and gulped. "D-Dai?" he stuttered.

"That explains your repeated disappearances," Amora remarked. "It seems that you have a lot to explain to us, Lukainy. Wing will need his rest, and I can tell by your tears that your journey has been too much to bear with the few that know the truth."

The princess struggled to keep her composure but replied calmly, "It's a long story."

"It's a long way back to the palace," Amora prodded while she organized her supplies.

In the meantime, Dai moved to hoist Wing onto his back, but the human-masked razor was stopped by Ashton, who brushed the sword aside and dropped to his knee. "I will carry him."

Acceptance...[9]

Book 1 – Episode 8

The night air grew thick with the sounds of moist meat being devoured by yearning mouths. Seven soldiers rested atop a bridge crossing the river border between the Kingdom of Cartheim and the Kingdom of Tistal. Aside from the smacking of lips and the laughs that accompanied the group's feast, little noise and few persons stirred the silence that covered the Settlement of the Southern Tier. The armor-clad warriors that bore the seal of Adrian's domain discovered no resistance within the village except from the young man that now served as the Hapsburg 7th's main course.

"Remember what I said," Rachael spoke softly, her hushed tone pulsing with authority. "I only let you kill this one because the boy will be mine to entertain." Her crimson glare targeted each member of the 7th – excluding one who dawdled on the outskirts of the cluster – and her pallid fangs glimmered under the sickle moon.

The laughs dwindled before five individuals looked to Wolfe. "That is fine with me," a flaxen woman responded. "This one's blood will suffice." She smirked and held a crystal chalice to the sky while darkened orbs lingered upon the paintings of life that coated the rim. "Six-hundred one," she muttered while a trio of men grew increasingly irritated.

"What is wrong with the three of you?" Rachael interrupted the groaning. "Erzse is satisfied with her share of this kill, but you dogs are pissing like babies over your lots. Need I remind you that Lord Conrad is counting on us? No one should take the chance of tempting my impatience when the stakes could not be any higher. Don't forget that all of your souls are ensnared by my flame; I have no problem with acquiring fulfillment from my pets."

A scrawny man with lust consuming every bit of his olive-decorated oculars scoffed Wolfe's threats as a wad of his spit hit the bridge timber. "If Peter hadn't killed him that fast, then we could have all had our fun," he roared, glancing at the brown-haired, self-proclaimed werewolf. He dug his long fingers into the eviscerated torso and showed his bloodstained claws to the heavens. "What good is the blood if the suffering ends before satisfaction?"

With an icy, blue-eyed scowl, Peter Stumpp replied in a husky voice, "It's not my fault it takes you longer than five minutes! Enjoy the corpse, Ruhr; it's delicious even when you don't shoot the load." He gave a one-breath chuckle and glimpsed at Rachael's ruby cores. "Don't even think that I am complaining." He licked his teeth and moaned at bits of flesh that the tip of his tongue retrieved. "I'm with Erzse; this guy was sweet – like a dessert."

A scarred hand cradled the head of the victim, and brown eyes gazed upon the retracted, lifeless irides that served as reticules to highlight the netherworld. "He was cute," Raab Fritz spoke faintly as his other hand parted thin black strands of hair. "I don't care about either of your arguments," he informed and turned his head from Peter to Ruhr. "I would much rather play with Fox, but someone won't let me have the opportunity."

"If Rachael let you have the opportunity," the outsider countered, "then I would kill you." The teen stepped towards the pack and scowled at Raab with piercing maroon orbs before Wolfe rose to her feet and took hold of the boy's scruffy red hair.

"Calm down, runt," she ordered and pushed the snarling Fox aside. Despite his desire to crush Fritz, Fox Wusten could tell when his mistress was irritated and dangerous. He was one of the few that knew the truth about Rachael Wolfe; harbored beneath hide with twenty years of wear, lurked a witch with cruel wisdom and seductive powers that blossomed for generations. "Raab, Ruhr," she said, her body floating towards the two men.

They froze to her voice – that siren's call saturated with a vicious sweetness that made sweat drip from every pore. "Yes?" they replied as chilling shivers rolled up and down their spines.

"Did you finish your missions today?" she cooed while continuing her slow advance. Perspiration beaded around their necks when they nodded, uncontrolled pants escaped their lips when Rachael pressed her hands against their thighs, and Fox smirked when the view of Wolfe's figure made Raab and Ruhr helpless to their base pleasures. "That's good," she responded in an overly feminine tone. Her fingers crawled upon wavering skin in a sadistic victory parade over captured ground. Blood began oozing from the men's eyes for the witch's spell – a menacing curse that warped the wants and needs of the human imagination into a ravaging disease – had already been cast.

Ruhr Kurten did not move from the cold claws that severed his head. Instead, his pupils merely rolled back into the skull and his mouth hung open to emit silent wails in appreciation for the deliverance of his greatest pleasure: to hear the fluid gushing from the stump of his neck. "I hate bitches," Rachael continued before glaring at Fritz, "and I hate babysitting men that I no longer need." She grinned and whispered into his ear. "Jump for me and maybe I will let you play with Fox."

The man muttered gibberish and crawled towards the edge of the structure. *Wüstenfuchs,* he thought as nails struggled into the wood, *is a glorious promise.* Images of torturing the boy blinded his mind and Wolfe's sweet song drove him ever closer to the plunge. Like a discarded ragdoll, he slipped away and fell to the rocks that towered above the water. His limbs, pendulums ticking away the seconds after death, dangled, and his succulent juices dribbled down the damp, jagged peaks to find the depths of hell.

The quiet member of the Hapsburg 7th decided to speak. For the most part, he let his enormous hammer-capped pike shout his words, but such a display from his leader prompted uttered respect. His yellow irides affixed to Rachael's freezing demeanor, and his tongue licked long fangs that grew well beyond his lips. "You always have your way with inadequate soldiers," Tepesch spoke.

Wolfe looked at the bald, muscular monster and smiled at *The Impaler's* approval. "I am glad you appreciate the effort I make to take out the garbage." She paused and turned towards the east. "I will detonate the bombs at dawn; I've always wondered what type of beautiful portrait smoke could draw against the rising sun."[10]

Beneath the same moon, four travelers gathered around a resting boy and a fire that shined vibrantly against the blackened countryside. Silver stems caught the night breeze and playfully rode over the pair of lilac blossoms that refused to look at anything other than Wing's still body. "I am not sure why I was created," Dai explained, "but I do know that Wing summoned me on the day he met Lukainy. It seems that the two were destined to meet and that I was destined to be his sword."

Dai paused and brushed his leather clothing. It had been a long time since he had spoken openly with people outside the knight's circle of trust, and he could not help but speculate if McCallister would approve the discussion. "But that did not answer your question, Ashton," he restarted diffidently while his hands continued to fidget with his robes. "There are several reasons why Wing kept my identity a secret. The first is that – given his history as a thief – many of the students would have probably assumed that I was stolen. As few noble families agreed with the admission decision, he deduced that minimizing such a setback was the optimal course of action.

"The second reason is that I could fill in as a training partner when the other students refused. It's too bad that you all shunned him. I do not think there is a single person in the palace that could fight a soul-forge for as long as he can."

"And Wing just kept coming back for more," Amora interrupted in a quiet tone. She was huddled between Luky and Ashton and kept half her face buried beneath the collar of her uniform as if to hide from the socially painful elements of Daizer's story.

"Personally, I think he kept it a secret because I had achieved the standing that he deserves. Maybe, through me, Wing could get the popular student status that everyone wants but few ever attain." The sword chuckled and scratched the back of his head. "I guess I should desire less shallow behavior from my partner, but he is a human."

"Is he?" Ashton asked before receiving a swift smack across the back from his sister. "What?" he roared. "I am not trying to degrade Wing! I get it, already; I did not give him a chance when I should have, but I wanted to protect Lukainy! Is there something wrong with that?" He huffed and looked away before Luky's repressed giggles escaped.

"It's okay, Amora," the princess replied. "I was scared when I saw him like that too." She glanced at the sleeping Wing and blushed when her lips spread to form a sheepish smile. "We all probably have questions that need answers."

Dai nodded and continued. "He is definitely human; although, it seems that his soul is really a chimera. From what Prince Christopher has told me, Wing was born on the same night the city of Cartheim burned to the ground. It was not only the day that Trigger reportedly lost his greatest weapon; it was the day that he died. It is likely that the forces at play that night had unfinished business and tied Trigger's quintessence to the one of a newborn child. Wing is really the rightful King of Cartheim, and the reason why he saved Lukainy seven years ago is because her psyche was fused with that belonging to Trigger's love."

By the time Dai finished the tale, Ashton had fallen into the catacombs of introspection. During every instance that he and the others harassed Wing, on the numerous occasions when they belittled his past, and through the many moments in history that they dedicated to the growth of hatred, the target had always been the Battle Flame. The blade was correct; had the same story been told ahead of McCallister's heroics, Ashton would have called it a fantasy woven from the strongest fabric of lies. However, the characters he saw drawn upon Wing's skin were scripted by the pen of truth.

Amora and Luky had released their tears. The former did so to repent for her sins; she was not an innocent bystander in this quarrel, for she doubted Wing's place at the castle just has much as everyone else. The princess, conversely, cried for a much different reason. While Luka knew that Lutti dwelled within her, Dai's words cracked the foundation upon which an entire life had been built. Her strength – her inner fortress – could not survive atop shaky ground; thus, with a timid voice, she pitched her emotional mortar at the fissures and let her feelings be known. "Does that mean that I love Wing because Lutti loves him?"

Dai blinked and crawled past the group towards the distraught girl. "I cannot answer that question for you, milady," he said after placing his hands firmly on her shoulders. "That is a question directed towards your heart, and only it can give the reply. However, I doubt that you and he could have made it this far together if your love was not really yours. He needs you to protect him and would not have it any other way." The soul-forge turned to the Hunter pair. "As long as I am giving advice, I would recommend that you do not tell this story to anyone else. Considering recent arrivals and events…" He stopped and felt the locket that pressed against his chest. Within its cold, metal grip, Lara's heart rested alongside a future that guaranteed great trials and danger. "Just act as though nothing changed at all."

Frantic soldiers and personnel barked information as they ran throughout the castle corridors. Their worried wails echoed off the daunting stone walls and produced a droning white noise that annoyed Kit more than anything in his recent memory. An afternoon that he believed to be relaxing turned into a nightmare when reports trickled in that a group of Cartheim warriors had set the Southern Tier Settlement ablaze.

It makes sense that Ereint would wish to see me in these circumstances, he thought, *but I fear that this is related to that special assignment. This is straight out of the Cartheim War playbook. Why do you want Wing to go, and what makes you think that he will leave without asking questions?* Kit threw open the doors to Ereint's chamber and was immediately filled with disgust. Standing next to the throne was the short, stout, gray-haired weasel of a man that had scratched his way into the headmaster position. He was a nuisance that had opposed Wing's appointment since day number one. "King Ereint, Headmaster Argo…"

"This is a very serious situation, Prince Christopher," Ereint began after rising from the throne. "If these reports are true, then it will be hard for me to consider it anything other than an act of war. For seven years, we have existed side-by-side in peace, but to think or hope that my people will not react is foolish."

"The defenders of Cartheim would never break their oath to our peace," Kit replied, standing firmly against words that clearly could not belong to his friend. "These reports also state that both sides of the village were burned. Why would my countrymen burn their own town when it would only deliver them to the wrath of my father?"

Headmaster Argo stepped forward and gazed at Kit harshly. His brown orbs appeared to leak arrogance, and his luxuriant lavender robes floated in an aura of unearned clout. "King Ereint knows these things," he rejoined, "and that is why he has ordered the runners to preserve secrecy until we gather more facts."

"You are to inform Wing that he is to head south to collect intelligence and to eradicate those involved with this attack. Since soldiers are stationed along the way, I see no need to send additional men. From discussions with Argo, it is my decree that to repay the debts stemming from his assault of another student, McCallister must complete this mission."

"You cannot be serious," Kit interjected. "This is not a mission for a trainee; this is a mission for an experienced veteran. With all due respect, King Ereint, you cannot expect me to give an order…"

"You will give the order," Argo interrupted. "The Kingdom of Tistal has been ridiculed ever since that thug gained admission. Thankfully, the king has started to see the problems that arise when royalty is tainted. If you do not deliver Wing's orders, then he will no longer be welcome to train within my walls."

"Is that what you really want, sire?" Kit asked. "Is that how you are going to repay the thief who stole your daughter's life from the hands of death?"

"Deliver…" Ereint murmured while his hands clutched the side of his head. He struggled to give his daughter the happiness she craved, but the excruciating pain that harnessed his mind was unbreakable. Quickly, Conrad regained control of his puppet and masterfully pulled the strings of greed to return the king to a towering and dominating posture. "Deliver the orders," Ereint continued for his psyche was thoroughly defeated.

Wing, Lukainy, Ashton, and Amora stood at attention in the courtyard while Kit read the commands. The final nail was driven into a coffin that contained years of joy by sentences that provided a horrific exclamation point to a trip that had revealed unforeseen challenges. The whole way home, Wing and Luky played about an awkward silence that bit at both of their hearts. The man – concerned that his love had grown afraid of the beast – kept his distance, and the woman – worried that their feelings belonged to others – focused her efforts on maintaining the monotonous beat of her footsteps.

Once again, sorrow forced itself over Luky's cheeks, and Wing grimaced in agony from the sight. "You can't go," she cried before burying her head into his chest. "I don't care what happened; I'll talk to my father and…" She stopped when McCallister pressed his hands into the small of her back and when his lips brushed her forehead.

Four souls were crushed beneath the weight of Wing's reply. "I have to go." He could feel Luky's grip tightening around his waist, could hear her pleading gasps, and could sense the insecurity dissolving her essence. "Shh," he whispered into her ear. "I'm sorry…"

"You're breaking your promise," she coughed and tried desperately not to stumble into the deepest pits of depression. "You said you would not fight alone; what if you get hurt? What will you do if I am not there?" She was falling apart in Wing's arms and struggled to cling to him in a resolute manner. How she wished that they could become one to strike down the obstacles that existed only to tear them apart.

"I scared you," he answered upon supporting her exhausting embrace. "I cannot risk losing control of myself like that again, Luky. What if it happens again? What if you come with me and I manage to hurt you? My spirit cannot take the separation, but the pain will be worth the cost if I can discover how to wield my flame without putting you at risk." He smiled and peered into the grays of her oculars. "I'll have Dai by my side, milady." Wing began to pull away from her and almost crumbled from the anguish that afflicted his love. Her face contorted to amplify the wails of despair, and her arms mindlessly tried to prevent him from leaving. "Please forgive me," he said while wiping the tears from his own eyes. "I will return to you." It was a promise that Trigger had made long ago: the one promise that he failed to keep.

Book 1 – Episode 9

Luky clutched her pillow and pressed her face into the gentle silk. *His scent is still here,* she thought as fragments of Wing's aroma snuck in through short sniffles. The princess was lost in a state of increasing confusion. Her hero's face – a residue in her imagination's eye – grew more missed with every beat of her heart. How she wished that she could ask Lutti if those feelings were hers alone or if the fingers that needed to touch him were inspired by events from before her time.

Yet now, it seemed not to matter. Moments after Wing's great betrayal, Ereint emerged with the news that he had arranged a marriage between his daughter and a noble that could protect her happiness. "Where are you, Wing?" she whimpered and rolled onto her back. "Derrick is going to take me away from you unless you come home."

Another knock came from the locked bedroom door and distracted the lady from her sorrow. She remained silent, figuring that – once again – her father or Kit sought to disturb her mourning. Luka hated them both. Her father had forced away the only man that she had ever loved, and even though the two of them had things to work out, she needed Wing near to quell her worries. To Kit, Luky dealt the blame; while she had struggled to prevent McCallister's departure, Prince Christopher stood back as a subdued dissenter. *He knew from the beginning that Wing would be drawn into something horrible,* she assumed, *but he still did nothing. All of this is happening at one instant…*

She waited and listened for footsteps to carry away the nuisance rapping at her gate, but no relief came to suppress the swelling, despised sense of helplessness. How could she fix the problems of the world alone? How could she fight without Wing at her side? "It's Lara. Open the door."

Wing fervently rode a midnight stallion down the trail towards the Settlement of the Southern Tier. The wind that whipped his skin and tugged his hair failed to strip away the stinging that tore apart his torso. *You did the right thing,* Dai advised, but the once sliver-thin rift between duty and love now appeared to the paladin as an insurmountable canyon.

Unable to shake the vision of Luky's tear-stained cheeks, Wing looked to the sky and mumbled, "Did I?" His hands gripped the leather reins of the steed and trembled from the unwavering desire to return to the palace, but he knew that he could not go back. "Until I know that I will never scare Lukainy again, I cannot be anywhere near her," he admitted and lowered his head as the guilt slowly devolved to emptiness.

You have to talk with Trigger, Dai continued. *I think the reason why you lost control is because the two of you were not fighting for the same goals. His voice has been driving your power since the day you were born. If you try to communicate with him, then I am sure that he will eventually answer your calls.*

"What if I don't want to talk to him?" McCallister retorted. "Trigger, do you hear me? What if you're the monster? You're the one who terrified Luky, the one that created as much war as your enemies, and the one that became a part of my soul without asking me!" He pushed – to a rapid gallop – the horse whose hooves founded the beat upon which Wing's crescendo spread across the valley floor. His boots gripped the stirrups as he rose from the saddle. "Why the hell did you choose me?" the soldier wailed and listened for an answer to drift by with the breeze. None came.

Even with the little afternoon sun that peeped through the windowpanes, Lara's scantly covered skin seemed to sparkle. She sat on the edge of the enormous bed and observed the dirt that marred Lukainy's blue and black combat attire. However, it was obvious to her that the smudges paled in comparison to the murky sea of oscillating emotions and conflicting desires. The subtle jerks of restraint that contorted Luka's chest, the vulnerability in her gray orbs that showed the chains of misery, and the unsteady hands that yearned for companionship were dead giveaways to the soul-forge that had read human feelings since the day she was made. "He'll come for you," Lara said, hoping to provide some comfort.

Lukainy de Marrok despised, envied, and adored the woman in her presence. A part of her longed to find Lara liable for Wing's departure and for the resulting sequence of events that led to her engagement with Defy, but another section of her mind clung to the prospect that she could find an island oasis of friendship amidst the ocean of loneliness. Her fingers played aimlessly with the frills of her blue skirt and she stared at the cold, yet soothing floor. "Are you a part of this?" she asked after clearing her throat.

"No," Lara replied. "This is Conrad's doing, Your Highness." She paused and took a deep breath. "I am afraid that it will not be long before Derrick will arrive to take you to the Mahina Chapel, but there are several things that you must know. Your father is not responsible for any of this; his essence is under the control of the enemy. Conrad was completely in love with Lutti during the last war and sought her affection because of her healing gift. Within you, all of her abilities remain, and he wants that power to guarantee his invincibility.

"I will protect you as much as I can, Luky, but you must promise never to stare into Derrick's eyes. Conrad will use the Enchantment Flame to steal your freewill if he gets the opportunity. It is possible that he will completely take over Defy's body during the course of the trip. I advise that you stay as silent as possible; he likes to play games through conversation and will probably be thrown off if you give him the silent treatment. You will just have to hold out until Wing figures out what is happening and comes for you."

Luky stood and gazed at the courtyard that held memories of better days. She wanted to return to when Wing first submitted to her affectionate tackles. She wanted to be free of the burdens that hammered fear into every decision that she made and uncertainty into every question that she asked. "What if I refuse to go?"

Lara shook her head and answered, "If you refuse, then Conrad will do anything to persuade you. He may pull strings to ban Wing from the Academy or – since he controls the lives of those he enchants

– kill your father as punishment. Either way, he is in the position to fight a war of attrition until he wears you down. Your best option is to follow my guidance for the time being and wait for Wing to come. He is the only one that can free Defy."

Marrok quivered and gulped. No matter what she did, her greatest concern challenged her faith in salvation; he was the one that had to save her, and her sadness only grew atop the ruins of her freedom to love. "Why did Wing leave me? What if he never returns because he discovered that our emotions really belong to Lutti and Trigger? I can never find out if those passions are my own because the person that I need to ask is dead! If Wing knows, then he'll have the same problem too." She choked and gasped for air as her string of questions and worries broke down into a frenzied eruption of panicked language. "What if he doesn't come for me?"

Lara took hold of Luka's hand with a reassuring grip. "Have you ever felt that another voice exists inside of you, princess? Have you ever been given advice that seemed to come from nowhere?" She held her breath for a moment and smiled. "If you have, then that voice is Lutti's. Try to talk with her and search for a difference between the love she had for Trigger and the love you have for your knight. Any divergence from history that you find is proof that Wing will find you."

Ashton and Charles waited for Kit to break the rest that disrupted the once thundering symphony. They gathered in a small, undecorated office with a view of the training grounds and hoped for familiar refrains from Wing and Luky to excite the palace. Yet the Soul that breathed life into their existences seemed distant as though its light bloomed only in the rarest of dreams, and the Hope that inspired zeal to burst forth from the unlikeliest characters departed unopposed to a chapel as if the unseen pen of fate scripted the tragic tale.

Hunter stared at the floor of the room and listened to his quickening pulse. The stillness bothered him, the inaction prodded the very core of his chivalric being, and his fingers coiled into his palms to release the rage. To him, however, the lack of honor that kept the others tied to tranquility sounded like a menacing howl. The shrieking silence tightened its nerve-racking grip around Ashton's throat and made his mind roar with a displeasure that beckoned him to the battlefield. He struggled through the excruciating guilt that bogged his conscience and begged himself to crush the painless pain that had pushed him away from the truth for too long. "We need to do something," he snapped. "This is fucking bullshit!"

Prince Christopher winced from the teen's words. "I know," he started quietly while turning towards the cadet, "but this is way out of your league. I have spent the whole day trying to figure out what I can do without starting a war and without endangering the lives at risk."

"We are all in this office because we are concerned about the orders to deploy Wing," Charles stated collectedly.

The steady, almost soothing tone that radiated from Charles's lips contrasted with the passion that accompanied Ashton's bark. "But I know why the orders were given!" He pointed at Kit and continued the tirade. "You're the teacher and not the bureaucrat! You sent me to fight with Wing and now I know what's happening! You cannot turn back time, sir; you cannot make that lesson meaningless because from it I learned that enemies can become friends and that anyone can be anything." He leaned towards his coach and paused to catch his breath. "Princess Lukainy and Wing are clearly at the center of something big. If we do not act, then what do you think is going to happen when the lingering powers of the first war decide to deal the final blow? What do they mean to you?"

The lips of the chestnut-haired royal spread gradually to form a subtle smile. Beneath the blanket of anxiety that covered his emotions, Kit cradled the spark of happiness that emanated from acceptance. "Lukainy is one of my dearest friends," he answered, "and – from the day Frost set that baby in my arms – Wing has been my son."

"It's settled then," Chuck interjected as a firm hand retrieved ink, parchment, and pen from the shrouds of charcoal cloth. His ash-embroidered gaze dwelled upon the delicate feather that – like many others in the histories of unseen worlds – led the brave towards the serrated path of treason. "We'll devise a plan that eliminates the risks."

The moon – a frown that hung in the orange twilight sky – escorted Lara, Defy, and Luky down the forest path to the secluded chapel that housed the agony from chapters lost to the torrents of time. Trees and bushes that appeared to be aware of Marrok's plight extended to block the way, and the cold autumn gusts that swirled the palette of red, green, and brown established its own means of defiance. Still, the portion of nature that watched failed to alter the inscription of greed, for without the quill forged to usher in the new world, the spirits served to scribe.

Luka ignored Derrick's attempts at small talk and focused her attention on the heavenly companion. The bittersweet sight resonated with the full spectrum of the girl's feelings. The soft-looking vanilla curve left her with a sense of warmth that picked at her arctic loneliness, and the argent razor carved images of nighttime romance under the stars. *I miss him*, she thought and wondered if Lutti would hear her. *L-Lutti, will you talk to me?* Velvety, deep-blue tones caressed the princess's strained nerves with a trace of sound that – while faint – testified on behalf of d'Espoir's survival. *I have to ask you if my feelings are my own, but I cannot understand what it is that you are saying. Please keep trying,* she implored. *I have to know the truth.*

Wing's hands held the unsympathetic loam in a grasp that longed for Princess Lukainy. "We haven't been apart since the day we met," he said to Dai, who was tying the horse to a large oak. The soldier propped his back against the aged bark and examined the bulbous clouds that frosted the dark violet sky. Memories of togetherness flooded the empty canvas which the night had projected upon McCallister's ghost, and each stroke of the past left its mark in a vibrant color that made the knight dread the present. But the sands of time – unrelenting poltergeists that refused rejection – marred the picture with gashes of wine-red and black.

From those gushing wounds, only hatred bled to stain the virtues of loyalty and faith that Wing held dear. "You made me break my promise, Trigger." The line spilt from his mouth and drowned the air in frigid sorrow. "You died when you left Lutti behind, but I won't let your history kill me. I'll beat your rage out of my body and let the Battle Flame turn into fading embers; for then, I can return to her and never have to know why you chose me."

The leather armor that once stoked his ardor now encased Wing in a skin of doubt, resentment, and suffering. The fissures that consumed the happy portrait painted by the last seven years left Wing adrift in a sea of nothingness as dim and as saddening as the waning moonlit firmament. Yet against this dreary backdrop, the fatigued teen sank into the viscous abyss of slumber.

The void of colorless illusion was parted by two obsidian wings laden with feathers of effervescent fire. The snarl that joined the eruption shattered the cadet's *stille nacht*, and the glow that illuminated a pair of stabbing orange oculars revealed the bushy, black-haired bane of Wing's life. McCallister stood and gawked at his scruffy reflection through the chimeral cavern that bound their existences. "Stop acting like a brat," Trigger ordered in a guttural enunciation before peering at brown irides that had lost their shine.

"Do you want to blame me for all your problems?" he growled and jumped to the immobilized plebe, who attempted to move in the realm of reverie. "This is where things get interesting, kid; the only one you have to blame is yourself." The Battle Flame jerked his hand to hold Wing's opening mouth closed. "I thought you said that you didn't want to talk to me. That means that you'll keep quiet until I'm done.

"You're a blind, fucking idiot that doesn't even understand who the hell he is or what he is capable of doing. Maybe you're still in denial when you say that I was the one that scared your beloved princess, but you are the reason that you lost control." He emphasized the *you* and felt Wing's pitiful endeavors to escape his muzzling fist. "My power is an inferno that can be controlled only by one who wields it for the right reasons. You drew upon my essence for vengeance – as opposed to salvation – and got burned.

"Of course, instead of focusing on your own improvement, you mastered the nobility's scapegoat trick. It's pretty pathetic if you ask me, but I won't hold it against you. Love will make people do the shittiest shit, and, although you're not ready yet, you're the only one that will do. As to the reason why you were chosen, that one was decided by the cross. However, my take on it is that I owed your parents at least the future of their child. Now, when you're actually prepared to converse with me, I'll be waiting; until then, wake the fuck up, stop wasting time, and get the hell out of my mind." (Note: "...ya goddamn hippies!")

Luky could not catch a wink of sleep. The chilly temperatures that snuck around the campfire tongues and the two guards that owned steady emerald eyes did not keep her awake. Instead, the sandman's wrath was held at bay by the strengthening exchange that Marrok and d'Espoir shared. *Trigger could be a stubborn boy,* Lutti explained, *but I could always tell that he was a softy.* Thus far, the pair had been unable to ascertain a difference between the men that they loved. In fact, it seemed that the personalities of Wing and Trigger were mirror images born from the same mold.

Both were shy when it came to expressing and processing emotions, both fought for their beliefs with a seemingly endless amount of passion, and both wound up battered and bruised. *I bet he was a pain in the ass when he returned from the battlefield,* Luka replied. *It's almost impossible to get Wing to back down from a fight, and even if I do manage to get his attention, he somehow gets dragged into it.*

Ever try putting a leash around his neck? the Healing Flame asked. *I always wondered what Trigger would do if I resorted to such a trick, but I decided that it wouldn't help at all.*

The princess bit her lip and kept her smile hidden from the physical world. She did not know why she had let grief's rain pin her to seclusion when the hope that she needed lurked inside an internal temple built to idolize things beyond the flesh. It honored a dream that had to survive and a story that – despite the unpleasantries – needed today to be told. *I know I'm trying to look for something unique,* Luka pondered, *but just talking about all the things we have in common is extremely consoling.*

Down two different paths, lovers rest,
                                         Wrenching fear, tormenting pain,
But beneath the same expanse, both do see
                                       Hatred's gain, watch the blade take flight.
The lines written by the stars' celeste
                                       Firestorms of argent death
To guide them past somber melodies.
                                       Pour from stories drenched in onyx blood.
Where and when they make the twine
                                       Pens of the old come
To heal the rift of their chimera Souls,
                                       Encourage the new to make its mark,
The space crippling the book's bind
                                       For although thousands of pages live in vain,
Will mend itself from the Locrian mode.
                                       Their deaths will not come soon enough.
Sad but true, through all they search,
                                       The hallmark dawn of this cult has not yielded to the dusk.
More truth they Hope to find.
                                       Within this nine, all one needs doth lie. [11]

Book 1 – Episode 10
Hidden under stitches of night's reaching veil,
Odes to friendship rebuff deceit.
Lost to the will of the sword, they ride,
Sifting through keys for harmony.
Trilogy of music, [12]

Transcend the chaconne.
Ink the end to my Night Suite.

       The snaps of horse-drawn iron against rock popped with swirls of dust that accompanied the baseline of the pre-dawn light. Air remained filled with the scent of dwelling moisture, and the wispy beams of radiance that spread through the rolling forest hills prodded Wing's weary eyes. He had not slept since Trigger's blaring warning barred him from the sweet serenity of slumber, and after sitting in silence for hours, the cadet decided to continue the push towards the Southern Tier.

Dazed, he stared at the harsh void outline that divided the worlds of heaven and earth and wondered if that empty purgatory was destined for him and his counterpart. Those obsidian lines broke from their borders in hysterical scribbles that gorged imaginations' realities, and quickly, daylight paled in comparison to the cacophonous stare that raped the soldier's memory. "Somehow, I doubt that you will be willing to listen when I am ready to talk," Wing muttered before the sounds and chirps of awakening life jerked him from the trance.

You should have tried to get back to sleep, Dai scolded in response to his partner's weakened state. The concern came from the core lesson drilled into their brains since day one of training; paladins persevered on the field by gathering nourishment and by preserving sleep cycles. The razor could practically hear the intimidating tirade that once made his metallic spine cringe from a nightmarish psychological frost, and he could almost picture those raven fractals that gripped the paper upon which tales of death were told. And now, it seemed – with Wing struggling to stay above the scorching chaos that haunted his dreams – that they were riding blindly towards that inferno.

"I know," McCallister replied when growing logic began to brush delusions aside, "which is why I want you to return to the castle if things get out of hand."

What is wrong with you? Dai proclaimed in a furious barrage of varying pitches that punched the boy's already worn wits. *Look, I know this whole thing is hard on you, I know that you have issues with Trigger, and I know that you miss Luky, but your feelings are not going to stop the past from affecting the present. You summoned me for a reason, Wing, and now we know why; you are going to need me for this fight regardless of how tough it becomes. If you order me to go back to the Academy, then I will have to resort to drastic measures.*

Thick flows of apprehension latched to skin while tenor rumblings churned in Wing's stomach. Every time he tried to outmaneuver the ominous, repetitive deep, the inescapable future either razed his flamboyant outbursts or ignored his more serene endeavors. "We don't know what we're getting into with this battle," he said. "Since Kit could not override this assignment, it's likely that Conrad has made his move. That is exactly why I want you to go back if something happens to me."

The unknown is exactly the reason why you do need me, Dai answered. *A town was burned to the ground; you'll need my help. My instincts keep telling me that we're headed for trouble, and Luky would never forgive me if I left you here by yourself. More importantly, I'd never forgive myself for leaving my best friend behind.*

He held his breath in an attempt to quell the inner turbulence that only fed upon the sword's words, but such persistence failed to free him from the daunting circumstances that consumed them at every turn. "I'm just trying to protect those I care about," Wing said while his fingers wrapped around the horse's reins. The knight knew that his comments were dull relative to the sharpened intellect of his blade, but he hoped that the cliché statement would withstand the torrents of emotional and physical distress that appeared to rip the universe apart at the seams.

A light snicker nipped at the edges of Wing's thoughts before Dai's energetic punch line rose above the fading frills of his laughter. *And what do you think I am trying to do?*

The earth's soggy fingers settled into Lukainy's pores and held firm when the awakened princess stirred according to Alsyne's orders. She never wanted to fall asleep, but it seemed that Lutti's fantastic tales of the war that defined her youth and birth became sandman comforts through the midnight hours. "Your wedding is a day away," Defy said before pulling the girl to her feet. His boss had grown tired of de Marrok's insolent resistance and consequently prodded his servant to administer a more aggressive tactic. "Aren't you going to look into your husband's eyes?" he asked slyly.

Lara's voided cores locked upon the pair amidst the morning fog that still rolled over the forest floor. *Don't fall for it, princess,* the sword thought, hoping that Luky would have the strength to oppose Conrad's unconcealed challenge.

However, the chord that captivated her will transposed the timid slave of precedent into a boastful beast that lingered in wait for the unknown future. *Look him straight in the eye,* Lutti advised with a motivating attitude that began to lift her partner's shaken spirits. *Show him here and now that his enchantment abilities mean nothing.*

"I said look at me!" Defy ordered upon grasping the girl's chin, but the princess turned away. Her blouse that once radiated a vibrant shade of blue and a crisp hue of black was now stained brown by moist patches of dirt that dampened her lightly tanned skin. She tried to maintain her composure through the sudden advance, but still, the thought remained that Alsyne had twisted what Wing would have made tender into a violating touch.

Luka's warnings failed to dissuade her bolshie counterpart from repeating the suggestion. *Think about it,* she continued. *You've known Derrick for years and he has never attempted to take control of you. There is a reason for that and the snake fails to get it.* She paused and let the power of her enunciation drill into de Marrok's consciousness. *His type of sorcery only works on those who are broken, but you have the will to find the truth; that is a courage that Defy would never try to break. This one, however, is far more obstinate and dumb as a sack of hammers.*

Emerald sparks erupted over Defy's irides as Conrad fueled the spellbinding tongues of the feared flame. A vile smirk grew from the corners of his lips, and a sparkle of white flashed from the point of a conniving fang that emerged from the until-then silenced braggart. His fingernails dug into Lukainy's jaw, and his hand slowly forced the princess to gaze into his oculars. "You belong to me," Conrad spoke in a sickening, sadistic tone that slithered from the confines of Alsyne's mouth. "Kneel before your master and proclaim your love for me, Lutti!"

Shades of stone stood against the waves of dominance that poured from Conrad's essence. Luky took hold of Defy's hand and pulled it from her chin before her grin blossomed behind lasting memories of Wing's love. She continued to stare into the man's orbs and let her greatest foe enjoy the moment while it lasted. "Don't be stupid," Marrok bit. "I am Lukainy, and I will never love you."

Students oppressed by the blistering noontime sun stood at attention in the courtyard. Their confused glances bashfully neared the outline of Charles's figure, and each of them wondered why he stood in the place of their captain. "I will be leading the training exercises, today," Downie shouted. "After considering the implications of current events, Kit decided that it would be best to return to Cartheim to meet with his father." He paused and let his hands rest atop his hips. "This is not unusual; Kit has left us many times before due to diplomatic obligations, and I have always stepped in as the substitute."

This time, however, the circumstances were quite different; the cadets' bodies buckled from an unforeseen pressure, and the upperclassman watched exasperation trickle from their pores with each released drop of sweat. "What about McCallister?" one asked quietly as though he wished for the heat to evaporate the question.

"What about him?" Charles replied. "Wing was given an order by King Ereint; there is nothing else to discuss." Their quivering forced the senior to suppress a smile, for beneath his solemn exterior lurked an enduring child that loved to lie. Of course, the secretive meeting that he shared with Christopher and Ashton did not impinge his juvenile addiction; in fact, the operation that he helped create – a seemingly perfect plot – encouraged him to roll with the flow and let his classmates dawdle in the ironically blissful purgatory of ignorance.

They have probably made the turn south by now, Charles pondered. Before dawn, Kit, Ashton, and Amora had left on the road towards Cartheim with a canvas-covered wagon and a couple horses. He figured that a westward path of departure would conceal any signals that a rescue campaign could emit, and he concluded that the Hunters' absences fit within the normal parameters of a political convoy. Yet Amora's presence was not a coincidence; in actuality, the cart supposedly filled with Kit's usual supplies carried the medic's entire arsenal of potions, elixirs, and surgical tools. They had no idea the destination to which Defy carried Lukainy, but they did know Wing's mission objectives. Once the trio traveled far enough to the west, they would swing south and move as swiftly as possible in an effort to intercept Wing before too much damage was done.

The shift to minor came abruptly as towering plumes of charcoal smoke caught McCallister's wandering attention. By the afternoon, it seemed as though the fires that had baked the settlement dwindled to smoldering cinders. Yet even from that distance, the hero could tell that the town of aspiring peace crumbled into a desecrated sarcophagus that housed the ashes and the discarded ruins of the damned. The horse stopped as it crested the final hill over which the gravel path rose. Its head bobbed frantically from the horrific scent of burnt death that spread from the tier to the valley walls, and its eyes averted from the sight of five blood-coated murderers that waited for Wing's coming.

Mangy brown hair dragged behind the bolting Stumpp, who left no time for introductions as he charged Wing. "Stay," Rachael ordered Fox when her claws wrapped around his flinching arm. "You'll go last." Wusten grunted faintly, stood by his mistress's side, and stared with reddish pools that became entranced by his enemy's chaotic grace.

McCallister did not mind the rapid start; with Dai tied firmly to his waist, he vaulted onto his stallion's back and executed a running dive from the midnight steed. The boiling, adrenaline-rich fluid that scalded their muscles propelled the pair into a head-on collision that plucked the threads of fate. Time's march halted when bones cracked, when tissue bruised, and when sweltering rage snapped Stumpp's sharpened nails into Wing's tender sides. However, past anxiety's menacing clutches and pain's shredding edge, the experience held within Trigger's soul broke the corona and guided the cadet's forearm across Peter's neck. Ignoring the hot droplets that leaked from his waist and relying upon his momentum – Wing overpowered the beast and drove the wolf's skull into the rocky path.

Roll! Daizer shouted as lightning struck from the piercing orbs of Tepesch and the hammer he carried. The earth-devouring anvil was engraved with a grotesque storyboard that highlighted the accomplishments of the vampire known as The Impaler. The contrasting shades of gray chiseled into the steel painted more than dull, monochromatic pictures; they were battle lines drawn by the baser levels of humanity that captured death in chilling poses of crimson and flesh. The bald behemoth pulled his weapon from the punctured rock and gazed silently at the crater nestled beside the shell-shocked Stumpp before he turned his attention to Wing.

The hot breath of the dragon brushed over the knight's chest as McCallister avoided the massive chunk of iron. Perspiration built between the boy's skin and the protective leather that clung to his weary body, and each drop that escaped carried a quantum of frustration that pushed Wing towards his sheathed partner. The ground rumbled when Drago and Peter began a joint assault, and fingertips quickly found themselves caressing the worn fabric that blanketed Daizer's hilt.

Hell hath no fury like that of a vengeful beast; that principle drove the animal forward with every pebble-flinging stride. He cared not for the massive weapon that roared above his head, nor was he concerned with the wishes of his comrades, for his trembling hands sought one thing alone: refuge in the sea of Wing's blood. Never had he witnessed such a blatant challenge to the 7th's power, and never did he think that he would understand the obsessions of Ruhr, Fritz, and Erzse. However, when his frigid blue stare met the fire in McCallister's ochre irides, he wanted to torture the brat into submission.

Dreadful wails dangled in the wake of the razor's release, and soldiers remained mystified by the blade whose bite captured Tepesch's enormous pike. Peter's hands – severed – lay motionless in the road and already appeared pale. Those sharpened claws that glimmered at the commencement of the battle suddenly seemed to match the bland clumps of stone that now served as the altar upon which Stumpp's mutilated form fell. His cries, as jolting and as vibrant as the sap that flowed from his wrists, failed to bring a pause.

Wing yanked Dai from the clutches of Drago's weapon and dug his boots into the dirt before darting to the other side of the kneeling werewolf. *There is no way that I am going to hit that weak spot again,* McCallister thought during the towering monster's approach. The burnt-orange metal encasement that shielded Tepesch from the knight's strikes cast the image of a fortress upon the canvas of

Wing's mind. Without tempo's sympathy, the dichotomous pair hurriedly choreographed its final dance; accompanying the steps of one were triumphant, confident tones that complimented his devastating weapon, while the other partnered with light, quick bursts that prodded for strokes of brilliance.

What are they doing? Fox questioned from the sidelines. Percussive clanks joined the climaxing first movement after Wusten began to shake; finally, the pieces of the symphony were coming together. With every step Wing took, his hidden flame grew stronger until it equaled the twisted ideal of righteousness housed within The Impaler.

The cadet planted his feet upon Peter's back and leapt towards the smoky sky at the moment when the vampire unleashed his hammer's potential. Beneath him, the sound of pulverized metal exclaimed Stumpp's transformation into the sacrificial lamb. Entrails swiftly uncoiled into a soggy mess that spilled from a hole in the breastplate, and Erzse could hardly contain her delight once the scent reached her nose.

Fox jerked free from Rachael's grasp and sprinted towards the fighters. He realized why Wolfe's brother wanted Wing killed and understood the intense power that dwelled beneath McCallister's skin. *He really is the Battle Flame,* the boy reasoned, *but if I act now, then I can end it.*

He recovered his swing too quickly! The warrior's fear came to fruition as Tepesch positioned his weapon for the finishing attack. Such efficient movement from a bulky giant astounded the boy, and the miscalculation left little hope to sustain the fleeting images of Lukainy.

His eyes, Trigger spoke upon emerging from his subconscious domain, *are unprotected, kid.* Wing's orbs widened and he immediately inverted his grip on Dai. His fingers tightly held the silvery cloth wrap, his thumb curved around the decorative end-cap of the hilt, and his arm catapulted the tip of his blade through The Impaler's ocular. He gawked at the satisfied grin that endured Drago's mortality and observed the limp pillar of meat and bone return to the underworld with the legendary mallet. The spectacle left a chilling reverberation throughout the student's spine, but there was little time to dwell upon the event.

The stealthy Fox had intercepted his adversary and had prepared a one-shot blow with his cocked fist. Rachael and Erzse waited for the 7th's secret weapon to bring a quick end to the fatality-laden battle, but both were in for a surprise. Through his exhaustion and despite Wusten's speed, Wing managed to deliver a numbing

punch of his own. "He caught Fox?" Wolfe muttered while the boys drilled their knuckles into marrow-backed temples that could not bear the black, serrated confusion of fractured reality; perhaps the greatest battle she had ever seen – one composed before the celestial host – ended on a chord of dual knockouts.

Book 1 – Episode 11

Downwind from the tempest's rage, a pair of golden irides spied from within the brush that reached from the woodlands into the hilltop grassland. Locks of the same color struggled to hide amidst the shades of tan and jade from the smeared streaks of scarlet that wailed for the woman to emerge from the alcove. Her heart pounded for the prone Wing, whose still and marred body had been bound by a snickering Wolfe, and her mind worked diligently to preserve the restraint needed to stop the repetition of history. *It's too soon*, she thought, realizing that Trigger had yet to fully awaken. However, logic could not halt the overwhelming twinge that played upon the feelings of a mother.

She crouched and watched the two sadistic females of the Hapsburg 7th drag the unconscious knight towards the valley by his heels. His forearms had been trussed together behind his back, and the cape of Trigger's famous armor had been pulled over Wing's head and secured to his neck with rope. Like the staccato ramblings of the intermezzo, the sly, psychotic pops birthed from the tip of Rachael's tongue spread to the ears of those compelled to listen. Alone, each note merely suggested the brutality that would ensue, but to Frost, whose years of service to Cartheim made her a top operative, the percussive sounds linked together to form a chilling movement.

The clarinet giggle of Erzse complimented the building piece when her snow-painted hair parted to reveal black cores that glanced to Wing. "What are you planning to do with him?" she asked Rachael after a pleasured grin snuck onto her face.

"Now we understand the reasons why my brother wants this kid killed," she replied with a reference to Conrad while turning her head towards Erzse. "What could possibly be more entertaining than breaking the Battle Flame?" She watched the Blood Countess's expression change, released a threatening chuckle, and continued, "I'll kill him eventually, but if he survives my trial, then perhaps I'll keep him as my pet."

Dai stayed in his sword form and wondered if he ought to reveal himself as a soul-forge to the enemy. *Wing's only source of defeat was exhaustion,* he figured, *which means that I should overcome whatever abilities they possess.* He paused his thinking and focused his attention on McCallister. *But their psychological traits may end up buying me some time whereas acting now could cost Wing his life.* A storm of heavy chords composed of worry, hesitation, and doubt rained their tarnished brass color upon the lustrous white of Daizer's spirit.

Around the ladies, the blizzard swarmed with picking flakes that pricked the deepest conjectures of the id. Far beyond the bourns of empathy, where pleasure's life seamlessly mixed with the sporadic pitches of a miserable death, Rachael drafted her masterpiece. "I'll make him scream," she told Batory. "I just hope that he doesn't blow it when he wakes up. I want him confused and whimpering first, perhaps even a little defiant. Nothing fuels my lust more than a helpless boy acting like he's tough; it just makes them more fun to shatter."

"What about Fox?" Erzse countered. "What should…"

"Leave him," Wolfe interrupted. "He got himself beat up and can deal with the consequences of that on his own. He'll make it back to our cave sanctuary; it's not like he can wander off anyway. That servant will forever be trapped by my spell, and one misstep will only lead him to the clingy hands of Raab and Ruhr."

The flautist's trills and rolling musical shades erupted onto the stage once the reverberating void of wickedness carried its prey to the underworld. Frost had little time to waste; she needed to gather as much information on the enemy as possible if her comrades were to succeed in their mission. *Michal will want to know,* she suspected while sprinting towards the sprawled Fox, *that Rachael is involved again.*

A brown tank-top shirt that waved to the breeze fluttered while Frost's feet hammered thick leather soles into the dirt; her hands teased a set of daggers that were latched with hide to black jeans that snuggly fit to the curves of her legs, and her desires sought to ensnare the boy that could answer her plethora of questions. The amber rays of the sun dissolved the heaven's misty veil and reflected off the unsheathed knives of steel to produce a kaleidoscope burst of light that mimicked the mix of emotions scuffling to gain support.

By the time Frost crouched at Wusten's side, maternal fury had won. The tip of her stiletto dented the adolescent's neck and her oppressive voice dominated the timbre of the immediate surroundings. "Wake up!" she yelled after introducing her knee to the warrior's gut. "I have questions!" Sputtering coughs pierced the shield of sleep and tugged Fox to the jurisdiction of awareness. Coupled with Rachael's absence, the lady's strength and cunning bewildered the young man who gulped from the dagger's point. "Where are they taking Wing?"

Gentleness seeped from maroon orbs that became lost in the brightening afternoon sky. "You cannot defeat them by yourself," he replied quietly. "My mistress will certainly kill you for interfering." He stopped when Frost placed more weight on his stomach and grunted when her weapon began to split his skin. Her glare – equaled in ferocity only by Wolfe's presence – was undeniably terrifying. She was going to kill him when he was needed the most, and consequently, his limbs started to tremble. "Trigger cannot die," he murmured abruptly, "but I cannot help anyone while she owns my life."

"Who are you?" Dai asked as tints of lavender outlined his review of the newcomer. With the band prepared to reveal Wing's destiny, the sword could not remain a silent observer that buried his part beneath the masses. As long as McCallister was in the 7th's grasp, he had to rise to the position of conductor and direct the performers towards the climax of salvation.

"I was right!" Fox interjected, only to be stopped by the razor's voice and the woman's touch.

"I'm an old friend," she answered, "and I am here to guarantee that Conrad fails in his endeavors." The subtle twitches perturbing Daizer's frame indicated to Frost that her response was unsatisfactory. "Just like your father," she groaned before inserting a delay to let her intensity build. "I am going to save Wing because I am Frost McCallister!"

Tubes of glass – filled to the cork with various liquids – rattled as a wagon rolled towards the Settlement of the Southern Tier. Palettes of blue that cherished the contents of each vial guided star-boosted frequencies through the gateway to Amora's cogitations. The vivacious glow that scattered the gloomy brume did not lift the burden bothering Hunter's intellect, for if Kit had approached her with this assignment a month ago, then she would have refused on the grounds that Wing was nothing more than a leeching boor. Maybe her wish to protect Lukainy coerced her to act, or perhaps the things McCallister did for her brother managed to construct a rapport long ignored, yet either choice led to the same conclusion; for the first time in her medical career, Amora reported with all one-hundred hand-brewed potions and enough provisions to bandage a dozen soldiers.

"Hurry up," Ash grumbled at the horses Kit steered down the narrow path. His hands shook as the urge to rip the reins from his commander's grip projected a cluttering of imaginary sounds into the cathedral of his sanity. As his inner self marched down the aisle, the echoes of that suite pulverized stained glass images that depicted his reconciliation with the man he had to save. "We need to go faster!" he shouted before hurling a tumultuous stare at the driver.

"Calm down," Kit responded. "We're still over half a day from where we need to be. I'll push them through the night if they allow it and if you promise to rest." The Hunter siblings squirmed at the prince's annoying proposition, and both emitted agitated sighs that brought an expression of amusement to Christopher's face. "I still find it hard to believe that a single punishment changed your opinions this much," he said through suppressed laughter. With restored equanimity, the captain bestowed the moral of their trek to his pupils. "Control yourselves because he will not make it without you."

Contused, Marrok stumbled from the forest into a large circular citadel of white roses. Beneath the little warmth that descended from the crystal-clear twilight sky and amongst the swaying flowers, Luka almost forgot the pain from Conrad's mauling. Ever since she had rejected his claims of ownership, he had used every available opportunity to slap and shove her. With the monster holding the life of her father over her head, the princess had nowhere to run, and with Lara's loyalty to Defy keeping the brand silent, Luky recognized that no one would help.

The flickers of bright green that emerged from the aphotic mesh of trees alerted Lukainy to Alsyne's coming. She knew that D had lost all control to the cowardly beast known as Conrad, and it was assuredly his cacophonous voice that crippled the harmony of the world when Defy moved his lips. "Welcome to our birthplace," he said after seizing the dirtied collar of Luka's blouse. "Do you remember the last time we were here, Lutti?" the Lord of Hapsburg asked while dragging the back of Derrick's hand over the noble's scratched cheek. "Do you remember how you and Trigger tried desperately to save this place by burying the chapel?

"If only he had let me have you, then none of this would be happening now! This girl would have been born into my dominion, and she would never have gained the privilege of holding my affections. All of those feelings were meant for you, Lutti!" He stopped, began to squeeze Marrok's jaw, and wondered how much force it would take to crack the bone. "It is too bad that I have to settle for this inferior wench, but I have my suspicions that you will discover the fierceness of my love."

Holst left no room for the organ that bellowed from the confines of the girl's subconscious once splitting stems leaked their lives' dew upon her skin. *We have to switch places, now!* Lutti cried when she sensed the wind stroking Luky's exposed back; however, with the dynamics of that one unlocking question not yet inked upon the score, the rhythm's roughened course stayed a writ for the royal to endure.

Conrad tossed the ripped shirt to the ground and peered with wanton oculars at his humiliated prize. "It is amazing how far one falls," he commented as he clutched Marrok's skirt, "when dropped from the secluded tower of wealth to the position of a pauper's dog." The terror that had been contained by d'Espoir's guidance gradually resurfaced with every second that the serpent spent tearing the cloth from the flesh. He laughed as involuntary whimpers only added to the beauty of his aggressive refrain, and he joyously anticipated the salivating victory that would accompany the lady's physical subjugation.

In an instant, Lukainy found her naked body pinned to the ground by a savage animal that shredded her black lace undergarments. Her feet, still encased by resilient brogans, dangled above the flower tops as Alsyne's claws craftily slid beneath Luka's writhing torso. Slithering fingers squeezed captured breasts that poured firm, rebellious heat into Conrad's substitute hands, delighted lungs released satisfied moans after curved canines burrowed into the woman's shoulder, and the tormenter's mind became infatuated with the idea that her crimson ink could modify history's beloved suite.

"Please don't…" the princess begged as her hands pawed the earth and as her face delivered newborn tears. She was promptly silenced by a gag made from the strips of her own clothes, and she shuddered as soon as Defy wrenched her from the soil and held her back to his chest. Muffled grunts only provoked the coiled clef to lash into the few residual measures of tranquility that separated Luky's innocence from the final bar.

"Don't fight it," Conrad ordered once his lips had an ear to fondle. "If you try to escape your inevitable fate, then Ereint will suffer a tortuous and painful end." She froze when his nails raked her velvety thighs and shivered after the feel of fabric was replaced by the texture of a perspiring physique. The tyrant peeked over his shoulder at the horrified Lara and beamed at the hopeless expression that she tried to mask. "Don't think about interfering, either," he continued, "or else."

Dueling factions competed for the baton's ultimate commendation as each party sought to outplay the other's potential gains. One, whose frame had been forced into the muddy patchwork of leaf and loam, yearned for a knight to ride from the abysmal delusions of reality upon imagination's fanciful wings. His pen would craft the words of her freedom, his charming melody would obstruct the mounting march, and his compassionate touch would undoubtedly eclipse the fiend's brusqueness.

Keep hoping, Lutti encouraged her partner as Derrick used his dusk-emerald apparel to bind Luka's wrists behind her head. The breviloquent accents – while appreciated – did not alter the demon's plot; he drew his bow and violated the acquired instrument to fill the land of Mahina with penetrating screeches that withered any happiness lingering in the harmonic tones of Aurora's garden.

The unwanted intrusion caused the princess to instinctively convulse, and every agonizing thrust jerked more tears from her gaping eyes and spittle from her muzzled mouth. She implored the universe to magically carry Wing to her side, but as Conrad gripped her waist and as his rule over her being grew stronger, Lukainy submitted to despair. "He'll never come!" the lord wailed while riding her like a beaten dog. The personal triumph only brought mirth to the depths of his distant quintessence, and emerging sneers carried ethereal promises of complete safety for a loved dad whose will was stolen.[13]

Panting, Ereint crawled from his bed and hobbled down the night-soaked corridor towards his study. The walls, coated with streaks of imprisoned moisture, supported a king that knew his time had come; he could detect the hands of Death tearing the threads that connected his thoughts to the vile dictator, but such delectable relief cost a terrible price. Beneath evening attire, the invisible scythe carved insidious wounds that, while excruciating, left no external marks; organs, formerly respectful of the monarch's longevity, simmered in a marinade of stirred lymph that unquestioningly obeyed the execution sentence declared by Conrad.

"I cannot die yet," he whispered as he tumbled into his desk chair and fiddled with a piece of parchment. His hushed solo spoke to an audience of one that, draped by the obsidian-colored robes of the afterlife, inhabited the shadows. It watched as a warrior, a ruler, and a parent created his last opus with a quill that chose progress above recession.

To my darling daughter, he wrote, *I am sorry that I was not strong enough to sacrifice my wellbeing for your future. You have grown into such a fine young woman, and it makes me swell with pride to know that – in the end – you became a hero during the hours of my misgivings.* Ereint's husk deteriorated into patches of bubbling puss that called for the netherworld's minion to bring liberation; however, the grueling laborer persisted in its pursuit of the paternal *al fine* and deferred the impending instance with a retort of *D.S.*

Do not dwell on what has happened, Lukainy; do not take the time to mourn my passing, but instead celebrate my life for the good things that have come of it. The universe is there for you to enjoy as long as you keep your happiness. I am your father and I know where yours resides. Do not let him go, sweetheart. I know that the two of you were chosen for a reason, and the powers that govern this land of promise may one day appear to make the daunting puzzle an image. Just remember that the Kingdom of Tistal was founded upon deeds and not words; I expect you to fight the good fight through the tribulations waiting over the horizon.

My final job is to determine a suitor that can help you carry on the Marrok legacy. Faced with that task, I see it fit to decree that from this day forth – Wing McCallister is to be given the title of prince.

The scent of decaying meat filled the modest chamber when the king turned to see Death's veil towering above his throne. He was shocked to see flames of fuchsia flow beneath the fabrics that had terrified humanity for generations, and he was mystified by the single white eye that appeared underneath the solemn hood. "She's already waiting for you on the other side." The intonation was unmistakable, and as the great fear removed her cloak to show glimmering pink locks, an alabaster dress, and a decorated patch that concealed her right ocular, Ereint had to smile.

"Harmony," he replied before she stamped his forehead with the symbol of a phoenix. "Everything makes sense…" His articulation degenerated into a slurred proclamation that slid into the grave of silence, and his existence departed for the absolute infinity without a trace of ash.

"I will make the same deal with you," the sister of Defy and Trigger guaranteed to a library that had returned to its normal state of serenity. "I will protect them. When Conrad comes this time, we will be prepared."

Dirt churned around Dai's feet as he paced about the flickering embers of a dying roadside fire. The midnight hour had long since passed, and Frost and Fox slept in relative comfort on makeshift beds of clay and grass. He was puzzled by McCallister's apparent lack of concern for her son and was agitated by Fox's complete inability to assist them in any rescue effort. *At least we know he wants Wing to live, but with Wolfe still alive, it is impossible for him to act against her.* He sighed and ran his fingers through tufts of silver hair while setting his gaze upon the brightening eastern sky. *We'll just have to wait until she summons him to the lair.*

Nerves tingled when the rustling of straw and the creak of a cart's wheel perked Daizer's ears from the cadence of his stride. From orthogonal directions, the noises came to fill the artificial entity with a turbulent ocean of moods that were quite real. He crouched and listened attentively to the approaching objects as apprehension compounded continuously.

A golden sphere broke the sandman's hold and cast its impartial lens upon the developing situation. With a sniff, Frost sat up and glared at the rattled razor afore an annoyed pitch affirmed discontent. "Don't get your panties is a wad." The robust whisper evolved into an imposing announcement that corrected Dai's strained vision. "Michal Broderick is the one to the east, and Kit Carson is the one to the north." She stood, dusted her garb, and spoke quietly, "We don't want to wake the kid prematurely so go stop that wagon. Give Chris the current report, tell him that I will meet with him in a bit, and emphasize that we have the tools to formulate a plan."

"The kid cannot do anything," the deputized subordinate complained. "Since he cannot give us information directly, we will still be going in blind. All we have to work with is ourselves." Her decisive reaction – a secret that jumped from the precipice of doubt into the depths of overlooked faith – set the blade down the right path. Arrowheads of argent and the memories of a man that once waved the banner of the Hapsburg 7th represented the trump cards that Frost would gamble for the life of her son. The carousel clockwork that brought Wing to Luky's arms completed its jubilee cycle, for Michal Broderick – the one person who knew how to trounce Rachael Wolfe – was also the one who gave Wing his treasured scar.

"Six-hundred two," Batory mumbled as she chewed the dried blood off Wing's removed hides. The countess – a picture-perfect portrait of boredom – jealously scrutinized her friend's dissection of the lad. The fluids that dripped from his hogtied figure harnessed Erzse's senses and drove her to sexual madness. Hours earlier, the mystery that followed the teenager, the delicious armor that self-repaired, and the obduracy that ignored vulnerability kept the Csejtian maiden occupied. But with sweat glistening under the candlelight's serenade, the witch began to discharge her frustrating urges upon her stalagmite cradle.

"Scream!" Rachael ordered after slamming McCallister's head into the cave wall. She reached into his damp mane, peeled him from the rock, and dug one of her lupine claws into a fresh gash on his lacerated forehead. The smell of iron invaded Wing's nose with every hefty breath, and the acrid aura of the snares sandpapered the cadet's beige casing into raw, reddened patches. His brown cores, depleted of their natural blaze, wearily targeted the torturer dressed in tight onyx cloth, for his skull – held in bondage by a devilish mistress – had nowhere else to turn.

Throughout the nighttime hours, the unrelenting dominatrix shed the sibling-produced afflictions meant to inhibit her fun. Hormonal tempers, aroused by the prisoner's plight, transformed Wolfe's innards into a network of excitation that demanded satisfaction. She planted her shoe into the small of his back and inched his torso forward until he collapsed atop the stone. "Are you the stubborn one, or is Trigger providing the extra motivation?"

Rachael parted the boy's gimped legs and laughed at how his chin tried to do what his hands could never accomplish. With the snap of her fingers, however, the seductress washed her toy clean of his injuries and simpered at the revitalized clay with which she would carve a new sculpture of dejection. *Don't scream, Wing!* Trigger rammed through the neurons of the paladin's enervated brain. *It's all she wants out of you, and once you give it, you'll be dead.*

The mocked hero wrestled valiantly until the despotic Nyx fell onto her resolute slave and drew a knife to his neck. With his immobilized limbs, the soldier could feel the overbearing creature that made him groan for independence. "Do you know what I have always wanted?" she added to the melodious confection that dribbled through his teeth. Her hair – stained the same hue as the chroma of her sins – mixed with McCallister's grimy ebony jungle while her edge – deranged by the absence of a carmine glaze – cut into his cheek.

She purred incessantly to his animated struggle as despondent whimpers fueled her passion to chisel whiskers into his face. Her explanation – and the vexatious yelps that succeeded – yielded to the forte commands of the Battle Flame. *You've persevered, which means the cross must have picked you for a reason. We still have unfinished business so don't you dare give up. Trust is the key to our connection, kid. Once we find common ground, then we can...*

"I understand that you're drained, kitty," Wing heard Rachael say as she dragged him towards a large satchel and a rusted iron tub. "I can't forget that you've been strung up all night, either; by now, I'm sure that you can barely feel those muscular legs of yours." She reached into the bag and retrieved a pile of things that appeared to the exhausted man as nothing more than a blur that faded into the dim surroundings. Among the weak shadows that murmured the fragmented remnants of Gustav's original wonder, Wolfe found the ideal environment to pollute with her flamboyant and percussive ambitions. "Don't worry, though; I'll make sure that you sense everything I do to make you scream."

He barked when the taste of oak saturated the buds of his tongue and shook his head after the 7th's chief fastened the bridle of his definitive destitution. Her words, as sharp as the tools she wielded, toppled even Trigger from his perch of inner solitude, for as the union of leather twine, glass, and metal shard dangled before Wing's eyes, the son of the world knew that time was up.

Enamel punched into the wooden bit until gums bled from the intense pressure. Grunts gradually grew into shrieks that beseeched a mistress to halt her rapacious attack, yet the strap that Rachael wove through the guardian's tissues rejected the captive's pleas. While her hand healed the leaking lesions around the inanimate invaders, she cooed, "A little more." It was at that moment that the cerebral beast summoned her fox; Wolfe wanted him there to witness the terror etched into her kitten's swollen orbs, wished for someone that could comprehend the psychological damage that she had inflicted, and hoped that the trauma would develop a contagious characteristic.

The trumpet fanfare of dawn's first light prophesized the crusade's coming and illuminated the savior's cerise shroud. Cackling, Hapsburg's heiress gave Wing his final instructions while she pushed his mangled frame to the tub. "If you make it out, then you earn your life." Her ruby irides emitted the same hellfire shade as Harmony's precious scythe when she watched the boy sink beneath the water's surface to fight the frigid certainty of mortality.

With each thrust McCallister made towards freedom, the flagrum thread retaliated with dozens of piercing perimeters that generated undiscovered levels of pain. He pulled his limbs until the jagged trinkets began to tear through the sadist's powerful spell and until ripples of suffering bombarded the barrel's shores. The depths quickly sent the warrior to the amphitheater of illusion, for there, the descending notes of the authentic angelic instrument guided the hero to his innate wisdom. *You said that trust meant our survival. Since I've been dragged into this battle for reasons I don't understand, I need to see for what we strive. Trigger, what is the cross?*

The sterling quartet that sprang from Michal's bow sealed the religious canon of Raiga Touketsu[14] with a trinity that punctured Rachael's heart and with a Longinus shot that liberated Wing from his open casket. Seven years earlier, the concealed assassin fired a pair of arrows that set into motion the coming of Armageddon, but today, his aim relied upon a commitment to change, to friendship, and to a future devoid of Conrad's reign.

Season Finale
Book 1 – Episode 12
"Hold him down," Amora yelled at Ashton while she sterilized her set of needles in the flames of lit tapers. Her patience chipped with each jostle and bump in the overgrown trail that distracted needed

attention from the patient dying under her care, and her tolerance diminished with each word that she heard spoken by Wusten or Batory. The two – freed from the shackling spells that fixed them to Wolfe's side – recovered behaviors and abilities drastically different from those depicted by tarnished first impressions, yet Hunter showed no compassion. Their joy-laden tones covered her makeshift hospital with an unwelcomed suite that ignored the bitter side of the pair, for without Rachael's magic in play, Wing was falling apart.

"Dai, get potions 38, 42, and 79 ready, please," she instructed as nervous hands threaded mischievous strings through taunting eyes. The thin curves of metal examined the disbelief sewn into Amora's essence when unsure sentences parted her lips. "I don't know if he'll make it through this," she said with a fraught heart. "Given his condition, we cannot wait for a proper anesthetic treatment to take effect. Keep him as still as you can, Ashton. Once I remove the foreign objects, the potions need to be applied in numerical order. After that, I will suture the area as best I can."

Distant from the ghoulish gnarling that accented crackling sinew and overflowing vitality, the fortress of Wing's principles towered above the placid landscape of his psyche. The foreboding structure – a marriage of pearly stones with elongated lilac windows – echoed the patters from splattering tears. Alone, at the center of the stronghold, the champion – dressed in bleached robes – sobbed at the stanch purgatory that belittled his pact. "Luky," he talked through choking howls, "I failed you."

The room's gilded ornaments of chivalry went unnoticed by a man obsessed with the permanent oath affixed to his mitt, and the nocturnal flares of the Battle Flame did little to bump McCallister from the reverie. Achromatic textiles spilled from Trigger's shoulders as the sharpened reflection approached its crouched and grieving antithesis. There, the coruscating attendant of spirits encountered a tenebrious sovereign of war eager to give his counterpart the coda's husky script. "You're not dead yet, dumbass."

The unearthed amalgamation of mortared skulls and oxidized alloys ascended to greet Lara, Conrad, and Luky. Disintegrating foil slabs obstructed the dreary conduit that led to a womb of creation brimming with ciphers that scrambled antiquity's truths; tattered drapes, covering portals of dirt, delineated a fragile union that encompassed a rising sun, twinkling stars, and repeating stripes; and torn pages fabricated engines of destruction upon hallucinations that defied the logic of the continent.

Stale air nipped the bare, taciturn royal as she waded through the scraps of previous generations. Guided by the haunting glow of enchantment that ridiculed her tenderized constitution, Lukainy unwillingly made her way to the altar. Burning thighs stung from the rape that she had suffered, and they inexorably shielded love's gate once his music ceased to rest.

"Decades ago, my mother slew her sister in this church to become empress. She did so for the man who crafted people into things, requested revolution with a swipe of his pen, and published Mahina. Yet, just like Lutti did to me, Raiga Touketsu punished my mom because of her accomplishments. He sided with the children of Aurora, created the cross before he cowardly fled, and perpetrated the Great War.

"You should be thankful that I have given you this opportunity, Marrok. Your crown is a sham reproduction propped up by those who claim to hold the lineage that my family earned. With our matrimony, you will enter into the House of Lilith, and with your healing flash, any resistance will be brushed aside."

The displaced aristocrat drifted to the outstretched arms of introspection that sheltered her from Conrad's garrulous tale. *He likes to hear himself talk, doesn't he?* Lutti asked as the static berated their solitude, but Luka answered with only questions that pertained to Wing. The girl's dreams – dissonant sevenths that never resolved to tonic – went ignored by the present, for the miracle they wished to find borrowed devotion from the lending grains of the hourglass.

I remember when I had to take care of Trigger. He was always such a stubborn boy; at first, he wouldn't even let me look at an injury, and it took him months until he allowed it. I know, given the present situation, that this is not all that appropriate to say, but in a lot of ways, you have a closer bond to Wing than I ever had with my man. You are firm with him and have always known when the power of your touch was needed. To me, that is reason enough to say that he will come to your rescue.

Awestruck, she pushed away from Defy while Conrad meaninglessly muttered, "I do." Her bond with McCallister was something that could not be tainted by the musings of a narcissistic monger. From d'Espoir's lyrics, Lukainy received the strands of rhythm that beckoned her defender; he would come to salvage the difference in their daybreak, for only then could he enjoy her kiss upon his scar.

Meanwhile, the paladin studied an untitled book that showed its age. The cover – a leather wrap adorned with a diamond pattern of blue and purple – was significantly damaged on its front side by a fissure that dug to legendary names printed upon the susceptible sheets. "You're telling me that this is the cross?" a bewildered Wing responded.

"Generally, the people who know of the cross assume that it is a typical weapon with atypical power, but it is actually the screenplay of our very existences. When hostilities developed between Cartheim and Tistal, those in command thought that it would solve everything, for by writing in the tome, one could theoretically modify the fabric of reality."

Curious extremities courted the delicate paper upon which unbelievable stories were told. In minutes, McCallister had learned of his mother's return, of his current condition, and of the burden that crushed his darling paramour. "Trigger," he snarled while the muscles in his face twitched, "can it be used?"

The quake of rage shook the temple and prompted the Battle Flame to seize the teen's shoulder. "It has limits," he replied with an acute stare that dampened the rumblings. "I'm not sure if a virtual manifestation will be able to help you; even the real one would deny submissions that were written by those without a strong resolve. You need to find a pertinent purpose and use the right instrument."

Outside the bastion walls, Daizer dropped emptied glass containers onto the wagon's blemished floor. His palms – varnished by the same frightening fluid – cringed from the pits that ejected obscene ooze through sodden cords. From the clues left by Amora's frustrated demeanor, he realized that Wing would not survive. Hurriedly, the soul-forge fought to overcome the sorrow that forbade his contact, for from the bond stored within his molded core, he could hear his partner calling.

Mauve irides – embraced by the birthing sparks of the Soul – met the quill of argentum that Wing towed into his sanctum. "Dai," he softly said before guiding the pen to a blank page of the cross, "we have work to do." As Trigger left to begin the final stage of his resurrection, Fate's mighty binds dictated the paragraph that would stay the ever-reaching hand of Harmony.

Come fair maidens, noble men, poor boys, and meager girls; gather 'round and hear the words dedicated to the safety of all that we hold dear. For within the chapel that ascended above the sins of another, our verse hangs over a bottomless pit of silence from which the beauty of Hope might never escape. I will not surrender to the physical manacles that lamed me, and I will not allow the Ender's child to take her to a place without content. Healed only by the mercy of Lukainy's charm, I will ride the waves of the byakko's thunder to her side, and once past strike five I slip, the Beginning's son will gift the overdue vow of imagination's Wing.

The contending arpeggios of E flat and A minor clashed once Daizer's apatite devoured the entrance of the hallowed building. Clad by mystical hides, the lambent Wing raced down the aphotic aisle that led to Marrok's side. He paid no heed to Conrad's venomous shout and swung his katana to meet the interruption presented by Derrick's brand; however, with Lara's crystalline jewel held firm by the crescent razor, the magnetic chemistry of their complex relationship repelled the driven swords.

Tyr's gospel had made its mark...

Refined footwork channeled McCallister to the stupefied bride who witnessed her hero as he declined to forever disguise his peace. His mantle soothed her disgraced stature, and his presence refilled her emptied exultance. "Alsyne, I am going to beat that bastard out of you," the soldier growled afore an additional attack rejoined with the edict to capitulate, but the two, having only shattered the bones piled below their feet, separated without the clang of steel ringing from their cymbals.

...upon the Journey woven by empathy's fire...

Incensed, Conrad – wanting to make Wing bow to the coroneted omega – heaved the broadsword at his opponent's knee. The premonition of split marrow bolstered the arrogance of the Lord of Hapsburg, but he found no success in the fabled third try as the dawn's warrior deflected the onslaught with the pinnacle of his dependable edge. *Lara, what is the meaning of this? It does not even feel as though we are achieving contact.*

...and by cruelty's Ice, for...

Xylophonic pops accompanied the plane of the knight's knuckles as it impinged upon D's jaw. McCallister went unbothered by the circumstances that hindered their iron companions, and he refused to renege on his decree. Unemotionally, he dissected the jaded ferocity that bubbled out of Defy's irides, and coolly, he sidestepped the retaliatory thrust that shot from the snake's unoccupied fist. The residual nectar of acrimony that tainted the cadet's appendage alluded to the fact that he was not combating his dear friend.

...the Gift of war...

Relentless in his pursuit of destruction, the general jammed his rapier against the invisible barrier generated by Dai's proximity. From the chantry, Luky watched as her faithful zephyr dueled the flagitious boreas across the stalemate shaped by the ferric pair. That expanse – a vortex threatening to swallow either ardor or pride – pulled de

Marrok's concentration until it dwelled solely upon the fructifying purity of Wing's aura. Spliced anamneses detailing the inferno that had once distorted the boy's quintessence glided into Luka's consciousness; he radiated the same fervor that blessed madness during the fight with the bandits, yet in this hour, she knew that no berserker would emerge to eradicate his virtue.

...had only begun his Ride.[15]

"You bitch! You gave away your gem!" Conrad unraveled the enigma that kept him from the trophy of ascension, and he briskly threw Lara to the side as a ball of green plasma swelled around the tip of his pointer finger. He scoffed her human form, ignored Defy's internal pleas, but saluted his alacrity to exterminate a comrade; however, the torrid stream that he unleashed never hit its selected target.

Lara cradled Dai after his petrified figure fell into her arms. She trembled as the smelted steel that had made his back charred his clothes, and she blushed when the violet oculars that had yearned for her life sought her adoration. "I'll take care of you," she whispered before her sharp nails tore apart his chest to retrieve his amethyst core. "It's your turn to sleep."

The serpent had to laugh at his enemy's misfortune; Wing's greatest asset had thrown himself away for an antique that was not worth her weight in shit. He had become a useless, melted mess unfit even for use as a wall ornament in a pub. The crescendo of the concluding phrase infiltrated every snide cackle that inflated Conrad's overblown ego, for the sinister lord had acquired a defenseless McCallister as a stand-in bull's-eye for his enchanted ammunition.

"Are you done?" The blunt statement stole the tyrant's fun and dragged his lime focus to Trigger's piercing amber disks. From Wing's shoulders, spikes of sable fire exploded and blew the roof off the shrine 'fore they settled into an angelic pose. Both Conrad and Lukainy observed the five runic letters that – once burned into the back of the paladin's left hand – fashioned a true dichotomy with the assistance of an older pledge. "I'm sorry," Trigger tantalized. "Was that not dramatic enough for you? Let me try again, Conny; I'm going to whip your ass."

The Battle Flame lifted his arm until his middle and index digits followed the eccentric motion of the reptilian adversary. "You've finally come out of your shell, but what are you going to do?" Conrad retorted. "Do you think that anything has changed in seven years? You'll try to free your brother from my control, but you will fail again. There is no way to divide us!" The beryl fireballs that darted from the dishonorable dragon were immediately extinguished by a cluster of midnight bolts that jumped from the crafty Trigger.

"You're wrong," he replied after showing off his stunning aim. "There is one pretty large difference between then and now; I have Wing. Aren't you the least bit bothered by the fact that this kid appeared out of nowhere?" Trigger ventured on with trademarked sarcasm. "Do you want to know how he did it, Conny? He learned how to use what you really want." McCallister – the proverbial man in the mirror – positioned the pane through which Trigger could visualize the wires that linked Defy to Conrad's authority.

The dilapidated room rocked as a sanguine pentagram appeared on the ground ahead of the alpha's first footstep. The star blossomed into a volcano of remembrance that spewed howling spirits that the omega had slain. Their abstract song – a glorious composition to the likes of Luky and Trigger – vexed Conrad, for it was the chorus meant to deliver the medium of his defeat.

Gradually, a long, riveted iron box – equipped with five segmented bainite blades – rose from the depths of hell until the cap of its hilt found the Battle Flame's receptive palm. "Kouenza," Trigger acknowledged the soul-forge before pulling the sword to a striking position. He flipped a cylindrical switch that collared the pipe, watched as each silver edge sprang to a preset angle of inclination, adored the onyx blaze that permeated his weapon, and with one swipe, found Conrad's march blinded by the light.

To be continued…

[Adam's Info]

I am always mildly amused by the few people that come into my life that actually want to know things about me. When I looked over the notes section, I could almost hear my mother's voice ring in my ear, "Don't forget to include something about you." Oh well, here we go.

My birthday is October 28, 1985. I am from the west suburbs of Chicago – or as how we locals dub it – the West Syeeed. Don't give me that damn look. You know you've done it at least once. I love just about anything that will keep me entertained: anime, drawing, food, legos, music, physics, and – of course – writing. I also enjoy critiquing the literary works of others, which I have done since the founding of the AGWC in 2006.

My favorite author would have to be William Faulkner. In fact, I own an Underwood typewriter that is the same model as the one he used. Light in August was the piece that transformed the way in which I write, and I have strived to achieve the same level of literary excellence for the last six years.

As strange as this may sound, I feel that the goal of my writing was inspired by the death of my sister. Perhaps that is a little morbid sounding so I shall explain. Powerful memories leave everlasting impacts; I can recall that single event at any moment and still see perfect portraits. When people read my works, I want their minds to be scarred by the perfect portraits painted by my world.

Currently, I live on the border of Minneapolis and Saint Paul, Minnesota, where I am pursuing a Ph.D. in High Energy Particle Physics. Pew pew!

[Adam's Notes]

[1]: Originally, this rewritten section was made solely for the extended version. However, I felt it improved the quality of the episode, so I threw it into the master release.

[2]: MC wasn't intended to become a series. In reality, it was more of a strange attempt to impress a girl; this is why you have an awkward romantic – yes, I am using the term loosely – scene in the first five pages. On-the-other-hand, I guess it worked. ☺

[3]: Soul-forges are perhaps the coolest things that I have ever added to a story. I'll share with you my two sources of inspiration in creating them. First, I'd be a fool to omit Derflinger from Zero no Tsukaima. The concept of a weapon having a personality is just extremely appealing to me. In addition, since I focus more on narration than dialogue, an internal conversation between a soul-forge and its wielder allows me to add some finer writing elements to what may otherwise be a lackluster dialogue.

[4]: This scene with Lara and Dai stands out as one of my favorites. Not only does it promote the Dai and Lara pairing, but it sets up some key information about soul-forges. The gem that Lara removes from her body is actually her soul. It represents a material housing for what is intrinsically unphysical, but there is a deeper message hidden between the lines. One, she is trusting Daizer with her essence, and

two, even with the physical item removed, the immaterial remains free to ride the waves of fate.

[5]: Julie's favorite scene (I wonder why…). This page potentially made MC what it is. Few sexual prose pieces manage to touch both males and females quite like this one did. I'm not sure if it's the musical terminology woven into the narration, or if it's the vocabulary I used to construct this part, but either way, people just really enjoy it.

[6]: Most of Night Suite is made to incorporate classical pieces of music; however, during the Summer of 2008, I had a Metallica moment that demanded a sliver of my imagination. In case you couldn't tell, Episode 5 is written to Don't Tread On Me.

[7]: Trigger's armor design was in my head for months before I got to this point. Given the type of story MC was turning out to be, the costume needed to be sexy and different while remaining practical. What says that better than leather, chaps, and a little *300 jockstrap action*? Not a whole lot. When Raden took the commission for this MC illustration, he added the shitload of belts to the ensemble. It may not be truly canonical, but his modifications simply make Wing *teh sex*.

[8]: HAHAHAHA! You thought he was going to save her, didn't you? Originally, I was going to write a fantastic Wing rescue moment, but the lead up felt too cliché. Telegraphing your moves to the reader can create a bored audience so I mixed it up and had the girl die in his arms. Perhaps my subconscious channeled a bit of my own history into this one.

[9]: This is one of my favorite parts of the book. The dichotomy between Wing's insane moment and Ashton's emergence as a protagonist always leaves me with a moderately sick smile on my face.

[10]: The Hapsburg 7th provides that glorious window through which the mere mortal may peer into the deranged, sadistic world that only Rachael could inspire. Perhaps it may seem cruel to use one of your closest friends (and ex…☺) as the basis for a character who is evil and twisted, but there is just no one in my life more suited to play a seductive female bent on enslaving or killing whatever bit of humanity she can. In all honesty, she was born to play the role, and I'm glad she can take pride in assuming the moniker: the deadliest – and most feared – bitch in all of MC. With the exception of Fox Wusten – who is based on the German Field Marshal Erwin Rommel – the rest of the 7th

is composed of notable serial killers and crazies from European history. Let's take a look at the historical figures that add their own nutjob personalities to this conglomerate of destructive individuals.

Erzse – Countess Elizabeth Bathory: Born in 1560, the Blood Countess of the Kingdom of Hungary was accused of murdering over 600 people. The hysteria that surrounded her case and imprisonment led to rumors that she had bathed in her victims' blood to absorb their youth. Of course, this is not as entertaining as watching a chalice-wielding psycho drink the fluids of our favorite heroes, now is it?

Raab Fritz – Friedrich Haarman: Fritz was a German serial killer charged in the deaths of 27 boys in the early 20th Century. He was executed in 1925 by guillotine, which – while cool – still pales in comparison to being led off a bridge by Wolfe. By the way, I got the name Raab from the actor who played Fritz in the 1973 film *The Tenderness of the Wolves*.

Ruhr Kurten – Peter Kurten: Another German serial killer – known as the Vampire of Dusseldorf – that committed sexual acts, assaults, and murders against men, women, and children. Time to take a look at his ESPN highlight reel: he sexually assaulted and killed an 8-year-old girl, strangled and stabbed a five-year-old with a pair of scissors, and beat a servant with a hammer. Since Stumpp was cast as the Peter of the group, I used Ruhr – the area in which Kurten killed – as his first name.

Peter Stumpp – The Werewolf of Bedburg: Stumpp was a German farmer that – at some point in the 16th Century – lost his fucking mind. A self-proclaimed werewolf, Peter was sentenced to death after his cannibalistic and incestuous acts led to his conviction. He confessed to eating pregnant women, two fetuses, fourteen children, and his own son.

Tepesch – Vlad Tepes: The Impaler himself. This one is pretty straight forward. The beloved Prince of Wallachia, born in 1431, resisted the Ottoman Empire and did it in style. His punishments lingered in the hearts of scholars for generations, and he gave Bram Stoker the inspiration for Dracula. If anyone deserves a place in the Hapsburg 7th, it's Vlad. Way to pike them bitches broham.

[11]: Episode 9 is laced with clues that draw the road map for the remainder of the Canonical MC books. Of course, I'm not one to fully divulge my secrets, but if there wasn't some sort of prompt, readers would be unaware of this episode's importance. The poem at the end was thus added as a gift from you to me. Let's dissect its true form.

Down two different paths, lovers rest,
    ← Obvious reference to Wing and Luky .
But beneath the same expanse, both do see
The lines written by the stars' celeste
To guide them past somber melodies.
    ← Fate steps up to orchestrate an answer.
Where and when they make the twine
To heal the rift of their chimera Souls,
    ← Soul capitalized to reference Wing's Soul Flame.
The space crippling the book's bind
Will mend itself from the Locrian mode.
    ← The book itself is a character.
Sad but true, through all they search,
    ← Metallica's Sad But True is played in Locrian Mode.
More truth they Hope to find.
    ← Luky is the Hope Flame.

Wrenching fear, tormenting pain,
Hatred's gain, watch the blade take flight.
Firestorms of argent death
Pour from stories drenched in onyx blood.
    ←Daizer reference; he is the pen to forge the new world.
Pens of the old come
Encourage the new to make its mark,
    ←Kouenza reference (Dai's father.)
For although thousands of pages live in vain,
Their deaths will not come soon enough.
    ←A tribute to Cartheim's Cross.
The hallmark dawn of this cult has not yielded to the dusk.
    ←Aurora is the dawn; Lilith is the dusk.

Within this nine, all one needs doth lie
    ←Me telling everyone that the answers are here.

[12]: The first letters of the first five lines spell Holst. Gustav Holst wrote the First Suite in E Flat for military bands. The last three episodes of Book 1 are a tribute to his legacy as all musical metaphors in 10, 11, and 12 follow the three movements of this wonderful composition.

[13]: Despite what you may think, Luky supported this scene wholeheartedly. It's a sad scene that was tough to write, but I needed to push the bar in some way. Many times in my writing history, I have

backed out of a scene because it was something I opposed on moral grounds. I was not going to make the same mistake with MC.

[14]: Raiga is the fictitious character that created the MC Universe. It was born from his despair over the events of World War II and served as a paradise getaway from Earth's realities.

[15]: The Runic Paragraphs: You may have noticed that there are five paragraphs that have an attached italicized clause. If you spell out the first letters of those paragraphs, you have TRIXR, which is how you write Trigger in Elder Futhark. In addition, those italicized clauses unite to form a poem that emphasizes the Battle Flame's impending arrival. The capitalized words in these lines give some information about the corresponding rune each letter represents. For example, X (Gebo) is the gift rune. And you thought I did all that shit for no reason.

[Sketches Up Next]

Raden's first commission was absolutely mind-blowing. He took next-to-nothing and converted little facts and tidbits into this image. Seeing this made all the years of writing worth it. Wing's design is epic, Fox's passion is projected, and the band-aid is just humorous.

I couldn't let Raden do only one commission; that'd just be foolish. Once you find a good thing, roll with it and see what happens. This scene depicts Wing's first moments in Trigger's armor, and while that is awesome in itself, the background detail is what makes this sketch great, in my opinion. There are leaves, flowers, and detailed architectural ornaments. It's a solid job from a solid artist.

The 3rd Raden commission! Finally, we have a scene that made people cry. Coupled with the rape in Episode 11, this sadistic portrait marks my evolution as a writer. Prior to this point, scenes like this one would have terrified me. If my soul was morally opposed to something, then my fingers would not let the magic flow. MC broke that curse, and I am happy that it did.

Raden's 4th dive into the insanity of MC. He really took the initiative on this one, but I am not surprised. Who could resist the chance to draw Ashton's turnaround scene? Isn't it just adorable? If you think I said that with a straight face, then you don't know me very well. Amora and Dai bookend this image with their amazing presences. OMG H4X! It's a drawing with four characters.

It would just be rude of me not to include a few of the awesome sketches by Ookii-Chan (a proud member of the WAFFLES community). To me, fans drive everything. Without them, I wouldn't experience the pleasure of sharing my work with the world. Hence, they deserve a place of their own here.

We have another Lauren picture! This one was so epically badass that it had to be tipped on its side. In addition to getting a modern Luky, viewers get the pleasure of watching a bunch of cute, little chibis do whatever it is that they do. *Luky: WHIPS! Wing: XD*

It would also be unthinkable not to include some of Julie's works. Like most artists, she's self-conscious and doesn't think that her pieces deserve to be shown in this book. However, she helped create McCallister Chronicles and cannot escape her fate.

This is another one of Julie's tablet art h4x. The background reminds me of icicle flames, which is interesting considering Trigger's attack list. It also happens to be the paint job on The Real McCallister DVDs.

This doesn't show up at all in McCallister Chronicles, but so what? Are you seriously dumb enough to turn down the chance to stare at sexy, doggy-dressed Luky? That leash is mine asshats! RAWR!

At one point, Julie got bored with her tablet and decided to do an inked chibi sketch of Frost. Thus, with great pleasure, I present Wing's mom for the first time in this cute, anime form.

Julie told me that I couldn't include this image as an illustration in the book, but as it is the first piece of MC art that I received, it's getting a spot in here regardless. In my opinion, this was the scene that *made* MC. Guys loved it for the sex, and girls loved it for its sweetness. I hit that magic line that appeased both genders, and by doing so, I opened the book up to a broader audience.

Aww, Raven did a sketch of a young, chibi Wing. I don't know what is up with artists and the need to put band-aids on my male protagonists, but it seems to happen a lot.

She did one of Luky too. YAY!

Look everyone! It's a never-before-seen sketch. I wonder why this was never put up on the MC webpage. Clearly, I'm just being rhetorical. Kinky writing is one thing, but kinky drawing is a completely different madhouse that I don't wander into that often. However, Raden gave me the wink face when I asked him if it should go in the I&E, so you can either enjoy it or STFU.

Kouenza Returns to the KING

My P.D.F. Mullet   10/25/2008

While my drawings fail when compared to the works of other artists featured in McCallister Chronicles, I figured I would include the sketch I drew depicting Kouenza's arrival. Despite the date shown, this was actually drawn in April 2008, long before I wrote the ending of Episode 12.

This is a little sketch of what is to come: Wing in Bedivere Mode. If anyone knows the music he is jamming to, I will dish out some props. I'm full of funky fever, a fire burns inside me…

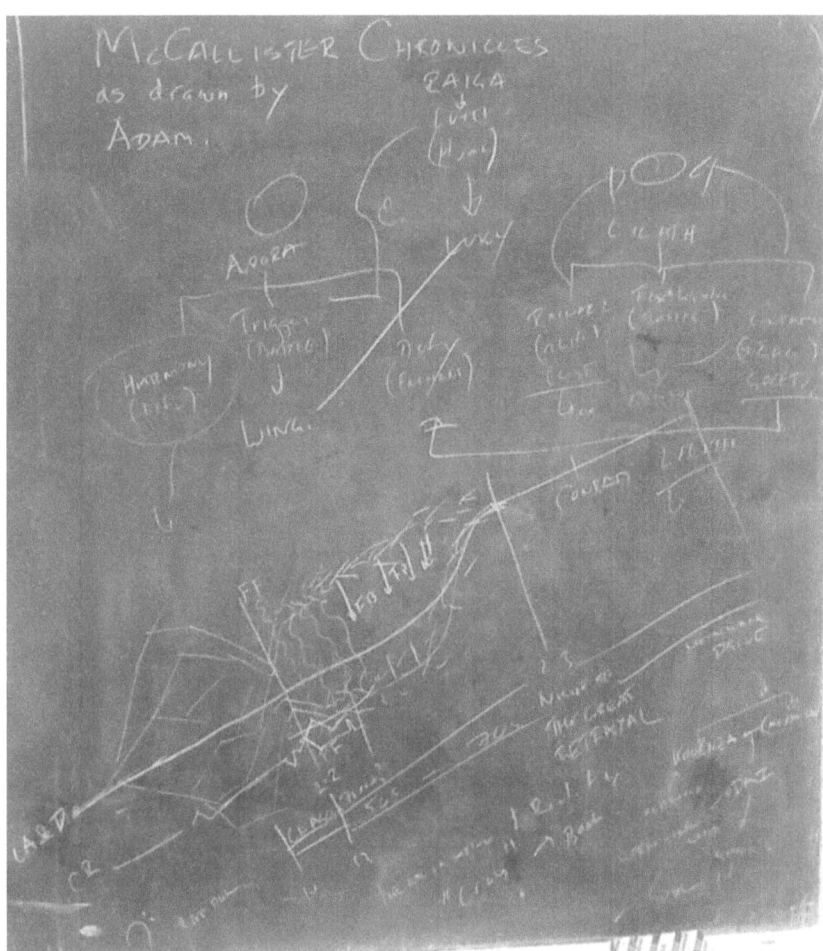

One of my colleagues attempted to get me to explain MC. The first thing my physics teacher told me was to draw a diagram whenever a problem is presented, so I blew his fucking mind with this little work of beauty.

[Additional Works]

This section of the I&E highlights extraordinary MC-related pieces that were produced by different authors. In order to write well, one must know his or her audience. This is what I told the participants of my writing contest in June 2010. The corresponding assignment was to read McCallister Chronicles and write something inspired by what the authors found tucked away within my pages. Included here are the entries that really touched me.

Callsign: Alambique
Title: I sacrificed my heart for yours

Her hair dances in my pyrite eyes,
her silk frame draped across mine.
Plush lips follow the boulevard
of my vertebrae,
she murmurs invocations of god
against the embossed cross on my back.

I am her religion,
and she worships the scars
ingrained in my skin.
They speak to her fingertips
as nails pirouette over the raised edges.
Imprints of psalms linger
on my wrist,
and her tongue traces the shapes,
quaking my bones until
they crumble onto the sheets.

I love you flows softly from
an ivory barricade
whenever her palms bow
before mountains whose color
invokes nostalgia,
Pinot Noir rapids
tumbling from your crystalline mouth.

Alambique's Commentary:
I got inspiration by one of the earlier parts, where Wing and Luky are in bed, kissing and whatnot. Then she says she only prays to him while looking at his cross-shaped scar. That is what gave me the most inspiration.

Callsign: Astaire
Title: Luky, with the Oculi of Venus

Fundamental interactions, supporting
the careful dance of our universe --
the collar *La Luna* wears
to show the Earth she's meant
to be his slave.

Wing, the steadfast moon
that rises over my horizon;
oculars pulled away from the sockets
to orbit my body, supporting
perfect gravity, just tantalizingly
far enough away
from the rotation of my hips.

Listen, slave, it's simple astronomy --
if the pull's too strong, you'll crash
right into me, and ruin my sweet
little system.
Maybe I'll risk the craters
and shattering moons
to make you *fucking scream* --

or maybe I'll keep your leash
just long enough
to keep you running in circles around me.

Astaire's Commentary:

So, I loved Luky's dominatrix attitude. Not that I relate, of course... Also, Wing, I noticed that you never use the word "eyes". You use every synonym imaginable, and you refer to eyes fairly often, so it distracted my inner literary analyst. I'm waiting for you to start using foreign language versions of the word "eyes" to avoid using the word "eyes". I did poke at that a little bit in my poem, but all in good fun.

Finally, I decided on astronomy imagery since you say you're into physics -- sweet deal, man. My man's in engineering, and he loves that shit. Also, I think the planets and their alignment have that connotation of "fate" to them, which I think really applies here.

Callsign: Maki
Title: Mother Fate

Three shrouded women stood over the universe, picking and prodding the strings, entwining some, while cutting others. Two of the women, the withered ones, toyed with one string, and the third figure, which had a creased face that still retained youth, looked fairly bored. This string, in particular, was just a simple man trying to survive on his dying farm. The fates kept throwing horrible things at him such as droughts and famines, and they laughed when the man had to butcher his beloved cow just to survive. The younger Fate just did not care for the life that the others toyed with.

She wanted a life with a little more adventure; one with a spark. She wanted someone to have a life that stimulated her interest, and she meandered to the part of the world where magic was very common as a result of the Fates' wandering interest. She watched as chaos ensued on this land, magic erupting and cascading as demons were released and then, again, sealed away.

"Madra, leave the magic world alone," one of the older Fates called. The young Fate looked at them as they began to create a new soul. It was something Madra was not experienced in, but she watched as the figure pulled the air, stretched it into a sizable line, and attached it to another string, showing this new soul's birth. She could already hear her sisters' plan for this soul.

"This one is a king, Ona," one of them said.

"Should we have him be graced, or doomed, my dear Ciel?" the one who yelled at Madra asked.

The two sisters seemed fixated on this king they created, but Madra did not care for this new person who would most likely be cursed. Her focus turned back to this new world, one that has long been ignored. The Fate wanted to add something to this new place. A soul, perhaps. Madra began to think of the man this soul would become. He would grow up handsome, strong, and powerful.

Madra focused on this image as she pulled at the air, stretched it, but the string was feeble and the life inside would not have lasted a week. She let the string fall, and it shattered on the ground; a life saved from death.

The fate went back to gazing at this land, and there was a fight. Magic was being hurled all over the place, and the powers of one were shattered, the fragments falling and fading into the world. Madra quickly snatched the fragments of this one's magic and began to create a life. Of course, it was a child, but she began to weave in special things to keep this one alive. She added a flame to this soul, a strong magic that would protect him or help him fight; a magic he would develop and use. She cupped this string in her hands and whispered to it, "Trigger." The name he would have.

The Fate pushed back her hood to examine a proper place for her creation. She looked for the warmer colors that signified a loving mother, but every time Madra tried to attach the string, it was deflected with an audible 'ping'. She worried her sisters would hear and take Trigger from her, so she had to be careful. Obviously, this soul was too different, too special to be born from a mother. Perhaps it was because of the magic that was used to create him, or because Madra had given him so much to possess, but the boy could not be carried in a mother.

Madra needed her creation to live in this world where he belonged. She found another soul: a father who also had a son. The life of this other boy seemed promising, and Madra thought this man could raise her child like the other. She tied the soul to the man, Sparks McCallister, and she watched as her chosen father found her boy.

"Madra! Come here and help us spread a drought over this country," Ona yelled. Droughts could be difficult to generate, and Madra did not want her sisters to know of her creation, thus she obeyed immediately. They sprinkled the brown dust over this country and the strings tied to it. When the dust rested on some strings, they snapped, coiling around themselves. Madra's sisters laughed and clapped as each string broke. Death was the sisters' favorite part.

Madra began to walk around the room again, trying to be inconspicuous as she wandered back to Trigger. The string was already getting stronger, thicker, and more colorful than those around it. The Fate could see that her creation was bound for great things.

Trigger was a fighter. He was getting into battles with other children, even at a young age. He questioned authority already, and Madra giggled at this fact, seeing some of herself in her son, but she did not notice the cacophony of her sisters' cackles had stopped. They heard the joy of their sister and came to see what she was doing at the magic world.

It did not please them.

They had abandoned this world long ago, realizing that magic interfered with them too much. Deaths were avoided, sicknesses were cured, and weather disasters were averted. Yes, there was chaos, but the Fates did not cause it, and that bothered them.

They examined the life string their sister had created, and they saw the power. There were more colors to this string than any other in the universe, and they could not allow this abomination. Madra pleaded with them to leave it alone as they brought the scissors over. She tried to grab the shears, but Ciel pushed her away, knocking over a city in another world. Madra quickly fixed it to be the fault of an avalanche, but when she turned back, her sisters were already closing the scissors over the string.

If the Fates could cry, Madra would have, though her wails of torture filled the space. She looked away as the blades closed in on the string, but there was no snap of a life cut short. She glanced back as her sisters continued to open and close the scissors over the string; too strong to be cut. Ona and Ciel were frustrated. They threw the blades down and went over to the world Madra had grown to love. They worked together to create a new string, one colorful and thick like Trigger, but lacking just slightly. It was a brother, and they attached it along Trigger's beautiful string, but the fates could see that the siblings would get along, their magic binding. They wanted to change this life, but they couldn't. Once a string was made, it could not be changed. Ona and Ciel could not live with this.

They searched the land for a strong and evil power and attached this to the new string, Defy. The evil controlled the brother, pitting him against Trigger. It forced the brothers to fight, causing them both stress, and in turn, Madra agonized over the situation. Ona and Ciel saw that this conflict would continue till one was dead, and either death would cause Trigger pain. Their work was done, but they continued to hover by, wanting to be there in case Madra should interfere again.

How is it possible that her sisters destroy all forms of love? Why did they have to revel in pain, chaos, and death? Why did they have to ruin things that Madra cared for? The youngest fate did not know, but she could not let the sisters ruin Trigger's existence. She needed to give the soul something special, something that Fate could not tamper with. Madra knew just the thing she needed.

She waited for her sisters to become distracted, and then she found another string. It was relatively colorful compared to others, and this one was a pretty different. She could see the power in this one, and she could see the beauty this soul possessed. She almost seemed too perfect for Madra's Trigger. But now, he would be Lutti's Trigger.

That is, if he could stay out of trouble.

Trigger continued to fight, and he was too stubborn to put away the wars to pay attention to Lutti. Madra didn't mind though. It was in Trigger's nature to do this, and it was only a matter of time till things worked out in the Fate's favor.

It had been years in the world, but it only seemed to be a few minutes to the Fates. Time was different for the two, and Madra was grateful for that. She didn't have to wait years to finally see things happen between the Trigger and Lutti, but, like she planned, true love began to blossom, and Madra watched as the strings began to entwine themselves into a colorful prism of hope. Their lives were now one. Whatever happened to one soul, the other would feel. Best of all, Ona and Ciel could not ruin the love between the two for it was pure.

Trigger and Lutti were happy, and Ona and Ciel noticed when Madra looked joyful once more. And, of course, the two had to interfere.

The two sisters were more experienced than Madra. They knew what pain could be caused when a Fate became too involved with a soul it created. The Fates needed to bask in horror since that was all that happened in the universe. Every life ended. Wars were won, but someone always lost, and pain was inescapable. It was just safer for the Fates if they loved the pain instead of the happiness. Ona and Ciel knew this, and they were trying to teach that to Madra.

They could see the love that had formed in the middle of this land, but they could not end it, but they could hinder it. They devised a plan, giving the powerful man, who controlled Defy, strength and knowledge, but they also gave the same to Trigger. Madra's creation learned about the man, Conrad, and went to end his life. The three sisters could see how it would end, much to Madra's horror. She did try to give Trigger strength, but, in her haste, the powder was weak and ineffective. Ona and Ciel laughed as the end came near. It was inevitable, and they went back to their games with the volcano over Pompeii.

Trigger left Lutti, but she followed into the trap that was set for them. The two tried to surprise the puppet master by taking a path through a forest, but Conrad saw the attack and acted quickly. He had a fire set across the woodland area and it quickly traveled to the lovers, trapping them inside the inferno. There was nothing they could do, and Madra could not avert their end. She could only help it pass. She created a powder of sleep, dusting it over the strings.

"Sleep," Madra said to her child.

Trigger looked to the sky, hearing her voice. It was a gentle sound that could have been mistaken for a warm breeze rustling the leaves, but he knew it was the voice of the loving Fate.

And he reluctantly tumbled into a deep slumber soon after Lutti. They could not feel as the fire charred their skin, as the smoke smothered them. They died without the pain, but Madra could not let it end this way.

The strings snapped, coiling around themselves, but Madra snatched the souls before they could vanish into the afterlife. They didn't have a chance to live as they should have. She found two lives starting that night. Madra used all the power she possessed to combine this infant soul with Trigger's, and the other soul with Lutti's. Somehow, it was successful, and Madra finally had hope. The lives of her child and his love would go on inside the other humans. It was the least that Mother Fate could do.

Maki's Commentary:
My inspiration: "His ears remained open to the voice of fate, whose gentle melody played in the soothing breeze." (page 10) Plus, Trigger's story...which is very much altered to fit my writing...

Callsign: Para
Title: Relationshits(sic) Are Dominant And Submissive In Bed

She gagged my will
and drugged it, hog-tied it in the scent of Amor
clouding over her bedroom floor.
Her nails poured precip-tipped lightning bolts
down the side of my face, charging me
with silence.

She laid me like a sleet storm,
out of reach; I pulled curtain sheets over my eyes
for a moment, closing off the sweat running down the sides
of my bed, and she poured her liquid body into me
until I cracked like a whipping boy
with the frozen-over eyes of one who wears shorts
in the winter-- body so numb-- I couldn't hold her
steady enough to read the fine-printed words
brimming over the ledges of her watery, gray pupils:
I'm the only thing knocking on your windows.

When she inhaled, she exhaled them
against my ear; I felt her chest against mine.
She light[eningl]ly traced
nipply, temp[tr]est teeth down my pulse
and drew a breasts for me-- bold exclamation points
that made the blinds on my windows
pop up.

Para's Commentary:
Lukainy and Wing sort of remind me of me and my boyfriend. She definitely wears the pants in the relationshit(sic).

Callsign: ViRabbit
Title: Luk be a Lady

If I was to do another curtsy and restitch my smile
where it's beginning to fray, I think the sugar
glazing my irises would crack and crease
and bleed down my cheeks like syrupy tears.
Then the screams clogging my throat
might dislodge, ripping the threading
from my mouth so vomit could pour loose.

I'm sick of frills and lace and *good day to you sir*s
and locking my aching face into cheer
when a corset's sinking its jaws in my ribs.
And I'm sick of lingering by the battlefield helpless
while your agony's flooding my ears
and images shove past my eyelids of you, limp
and broken in dirt. They get stuck to my pupils and no matter
how many times I wring my eyes out, the images stain.

We can trade, you know.

All I need is shining armor and a steed.
You can flutter your eyelashes and swoon.
I'll play your prince; climbing towers and fighting dragons,
coming back home to breathe fire through your lips.

Then I can kneel by your feet and press my mouth
to your hand; weave the ring through your fingers.
We can curl like cats on the throne and rule the skies.
Upside down heroes with nine lives ahead of us:
king and queen. Quing and keen.

So slip on my stockings and hand me you sword,
we'll have our own topy-turvy happily ever after.

ViRabbit's Commentary:
I found Page 29 the most inspiring. It's the part where Luky's telling Wing
she's sick of being helpless and that she's going to be his knight from now on.
Also, I apologize for the lame title pun.

Storm clouds – glued to the backdrop purple sky – leaked springtime raindrops that tugged at a long aphotic mane, thunder – tumbling from the skin of an almost-forgotten bass drum – bowed to the aurablist barrage that dashed from the knight's fingertip, and lightning – which matched an ochre glare – danced with a reborn razor that ripped sheet metal and severed toned limbs. Despite her majesty, nature surrendered to the ambitions of men that sacrificed the greatest gift to the thoughtlessness of powdered death, for the roar of cannon and musket was rivaled solely by the midnight sheen that proclaimed Wing's ascension.

The brush of Ares painted its masterpiece upon an emotional canvas already stained by wolfish tribulations. That eternally dripping concoction, a sanguine mix of ejected and earned fluids, protected McCallister from his pacifistic core with a motivating varnish that demanded survival. It dampened the numerous lyrics of loved ones – old and new – that still rang throughout the great chimeral cathedral. As chivalric as he tried to be, constraining formalities and virtues failed to fit within the limits of that horrific, blue-moon night. All that carried him past splintered branches, ruptured corpses, and maggot-filled flesh was the swirling, passionate emblem that tied him to an oath for one. Amongst the treachery, only it had been nourished by the blossom of his touch. "They protect me more than they know..."

A.P. Schreckenberger presents:

Dawn of Caliburn

McCallister Chronicles #2   & the Rock of Ages

Ejaculated slivers of wood followed the cackling wave of soldiers that pursued Cartheim's lost king. Hapsburg's army had defeated the eastern line and pushed to ensnare the remainder of the Alliance's defenses from the rear. Their souls grew tainted from a malicious beat that shat snarls of greed upon annexed ground; however, it was among this filthy suspension that an amber haunt returned to Wing's ocular annuli. *There is no way they could have advanced this quickly,* the knight informed his companion. *Something is not right, but I cannot run forever. If I don't stand my ground, these guys will run straight into Ashton's backside.*

Sloppy mud caked the corporal's chaps as he spun to confront the charging wall of camouflaged hell that tore the dampened atmosphere with metal hail. Smooth-bore bullets parodied order with swerving rallies and syncopated cries that nurtured the state of ambient decay. "I'll buy you a minute," the sword replied after a wave of released pressure broke the weather's cadence into a fractured spray that dissipated to reveal the soul-forge's human form.

Dog tags stamped with the name Daisuke Rekkr de Marrok dangled from a chain wrapped around the blade's neck. An onyx trench coat poured from his shoulders to cover a torso that would have otherwise been completely exposed. His silver hair had grown in the months since Trigger's confrontation with Conrad, and a cerulean ribbon confined the mangy locks to a bushy ponytail. Matching pants and combat boots completed the ensemble that sharply contrasted the benevolent, noble image Dai had worn for years. In fact, the only clue to his kindlier persona was the keepsake locket that housed Lara's life.

Pangs of faltered war cast sickly expressions upon the faces of those that witnessed the razor's unrelenting march. Their treasured weapons were meaningless in the eyes of the metallic warrior. After the abuse Lukainy suffered, the death King Ereint endured, and the pain Lara handled, the revived Rekkr showed no sympathy towards the men that advanced under Hapsburg's banner. He would not be stopped by their frivolous objectives.

In a snap, Daisuke appeared behind the opposition's disjointed front. Terrified shrieks slashed the pristine picture of masculinity as the sword felt a soldier's skull crack and collapse in his unyielding grip. Coarse, oily blond hair jutted out from the space between his fingers, and undulating irides struggled helplessly against the rising sickle tide while Dai compressed the man's head with the aid of a fragmented stump. Herniated brain matter joined the falling precipitation in a pinkish jet that sprang from the carcass. It marred Rekkr's robes with streaks of guilt that attempted to break the shell which time had built, but the spectacle could not wash away the hourglass grains that had already penned their scores.

Lilac oculars tuned to the trembling dynamics of frightened fighters whose shivering arms cradled smoking barrels that could not offer salvation. "Do you feel sorry for what you have done?" he asked after he spotted a uniform decorated with an officer's insignia. The lieutenant appeared lifeless during Daizer's approach, and the men fidgeted when the soul-forge pulled their commander's musket from his shaking glove. "Do you?"

Tangled brown locks veiled the deflated expression that culminated the career of the bulky military man. His chest heaved the dense mist into his lungs while allegiance boiled away the fear that the blade had bequeathed. He fixed his sunken posture to challenge the self-righteous scum that named itself both judge and jury, and his voice roared with pride as he saluted his troops. "For Führer Con…"

Daisuke slugged the lieutenant's jaw with the butt of the gun and watched the fragile tissues separate. Screams flew from the gaping hole that swallowed the lower half of the man's countenance, and subordinates grew squeamish as they observed a scarlet stream shower the bone shards that littered the soil. The officer tumbled to the ground and flailed, for shock had reared its sharpened claws to gouge and sweep pupils under their macabre blankets. "May you all wander restlessly," the razor spoke, having distracted the enemy long enough for the drained McCallister to swap places with his inner demon. "You've all wasted your honor for a rapist and coward."

Obsidian wings electrified the overcast sky with growing flames that defied their canonical foes and radiated ghastly shades. "It never gets old," Trigger informed the warriors, whose groans managed to defeat the drumming of the downpour. "Take notes on this one, kid," the Battle Flame lectured his star pupil. "Today, I'm going to teach you the benefits of inversion."

The searing amber flare that normally glazed his orbs cooled to an icicle blue. Flakes of snow congregated in the chilled fog, and the wet, soppy muck below his shoes hardened into a firm foundation. Fighters inhaled their frosted fates with each breath that pulled in Trigger's brew, for the arctic vapor that infiltrated their lungs congealed to create a galaxy of morningstars that unraveled Hapsburg's mortal coils. The cloudy heavens cleared over the Battle Flame's towering span to uncover a frigid moon that drenched the pyre pair with an alluring argent veneer.

"Every flame has its opposite," Trigger continued the lesson, "and it is the mastery of that reflection that makes a wielder unstoppable." He extended his right arm towards the band of foes and pressed his middle finger against his thumb to signal the pending finale. Beneath the lunar spotlight, the Battle Flame's brilliance swelled. "And then there suddenly appeared before me," he whispered, letting his thumb release once the moonlight aura lifted his competitive spirits. *Buriza-do kyouran…*

Mouths opened to cry and beg when tainted spears shredded the skin of the soldiers' torsos, but no sound escaped the tomb of ice that imprisoned the line. The first track of Trigger's second album ended before a hushed, three-person audience that examined the stained clusters of lung, intestine, and liver that were scattered amongst petrified limbs. Despondent faces peered outward to the unfrozen universe of the living with wounded stares that clung to the pains of judgment. "Wing," Trigger spoke, having observed the agony plastered to his victims' faces. "A soul with regret is useless here. The only currency in war is life."

Thick pants breached Lukainy's parched lips after she sat up atop her bed. The regal sheets cascaded down her body to reveal a shivering figure that struggled to remove the residue of a persistent nightmare. Oculars, hoping to find the outline of a beloved knight, searched through the grayscale sea, yet betwixt the hours of dusk and dawn, McCallister seemed to be merely a reverie. She sighed and looked at the blackened blob that was her chamber door and wished that either Wing or her father would appear in her time of need, but Ereint was no longer a part of that world, and her love seemed distant, even though the doubt was gone.

Waterfalls of azure silk leapt from Luka's shoulders as she stood, and her left hand clutched a couple of items from the nightstand. *He won't want to tell you,* Trigger's words echoed throughout her thoughts. *He was tortured and would have died if not for his desire to save you. He'll regret decisions and may even avoid you, but there can be no place for either of these things. A soul with regret is useless here. The only currency in war is life.*

"War," she said quietly, making her way towards the courtyard. Everyone knew it would come once the winter months gave birth to spring, for with the Battle Flame's arrival, Conrad's only choice was to dismantle the alliance of Tistal and Cartheim. Below forsaken rivers of blood, the serpent could search for the ultimate prize: the cross that dictated the currents of their world. With the physical book in his hands, Wing's abilities could be countered and the Hapsburg Empire would spread.

To add to Tistal's troubles, the king's death sent shockwaves through the ranks that decimated morale and crippled industry. It was only through Harmony's tenacity, McCallister's presence, and the R.O.K.'s summoning that the House of Marrok endured. Conversely, the matriarch of the household found it challenging to overcome her difficulties.

Her mother had disappeared without a trace, and her father – a compassionate and loving individual – had been replaced by Harmony, the imposing Life Flame. While the woman proved to be a competent leader and possessed a likeable persona, something about her did not sit right with Lukainy. Perhaps a hint of jealousy lurked in her heart because the newcomer had taken her father's crown, yet it had been made clear to the princess that her lineage would not be disturbed. No – that was not the problem at all. The problem was that this stranger spoke to her just as her parents had.

And then, there was the incident that polluted her essence with the worst type of grime. It was impossible not to recall the snapshots – those out-of-body negatives – that incarcerated her disgust of Conrad. For each of those stills that her metric devoured, the snake's darkness crept closer until she could sense its slimy timbre crawling up her thighs. It penetrated her flesh and infected her hips with impalpable tentacles that injected their anamnestic poison.

Ailed by this menacing apparition, Luky's pulse sped away from its usual symphonic character. Instead, it relied upon a rebellious throbbing – a fervent strike – that could divert the ache and anguish; unfortunately, such delusions tend to be blinding, and eventually, even Lutti could not heal the mental scars that plagued the girl whenever she felt the burn of another man. Panicked gasps followed Marrok into the post-traumatic madhouse, where digits frantically scratched stone walls that could no longer be seen, scalding liquids gushed from her violated physique, and emptiness reigned supreme.

She hated the helplessness and humiliation. Why did it happen to her and why wasn't Wing around to share his light? She wanted to grasp his skin and use it to scrub away the parasitic deposits of Conrad's vile aura. She wanted to make her man submit and demonstrate that the use of power without passion was a sin. She would cleanse her anima with his fire and dance in the tongues until they licked away the remnants of her afflictions. But most of all, she needed to show that her actions would be controlled by no one.

The turbulent freefall came to an abrupt end when Lukainy discovered that she had been corralled by Ashton's arms. Her nails had torn through the sleeve of his pallid sleeping garment, and four small pools of blood blemished the fabric. Shame reined in her emotions while her palpebrae briefly concealed thinned irides that broadcast her embarrassment. Only after investigating the tiny cuts on his arm did Luka recover the courage to peer into his hazel orbs. "Ashton," Marrok said to break the silence, "I'm sorry."

Hunter shrugged and replied, "Don't worry about it, milady. I believe Wing is in the blacksmith's barn. It would be my honor to escort you there if that is your wish." Luky smiled, having never caught Ash with such a down-to-earth appearance. His blond hair – normally groomed to perfection – fell floppily over his forehead, and the arrogance that once ruled his demeanor was not found in the caring embrace.

Wing sighed at the sight of Daizer's cracked spine. He had laid the katana on a bench before the enormous hearth at the center of the barn and wondered if he would ever be able to repair his fighting partner. Paled and dazed, the knight fought to stay awake; he could not dare sleep while depraved visions of his murder waited on the other side of slumber's threshold. "You have to tell her!" Amora shouted as Lara gestured in agreement. "You cannot go on like this; don't you see that we're all worried about you?"

Perspiration built under McCallister's leather ensemble as he stood by the shop's blaze. "I appreciate your concerns," he replied while removing his cape, "but I cannot tell Luky what happened." He paused and tossed the article to the floor before brushing the vest with the back of his hand. "She was raped, her father died, and her mother is missing; I will not bother her with things that happened to me."

Amora briskly stepped towards the boy, her light green gown swaying to and fro as she pushed up on her toes to look straight into his oculars. "She's already asking questions while you're off hiding from your problems. Do you even hear what irrational things you're saying? She needs you to comfort her, and you need her to comfort you. If you cannot get your act together, then I'll tranquilize you."

The girl's last sentence came off as particularly cold to Wing, who immediately gnashed his teeth and stumbled backwards. "Not yet," he replied, his hands quivering. "When I close my eyes, she's there, telling me how she's going to kill me." He looked back to his dormant razor and prayed that Dai would wake up to give him support. "We don't think that she's really dead. I don't know how, but Wolfe is still alive. I got away, but she's a serial killer, Ams. I feel it! Eventually, she'll come to end what she began."

"You haven't slept soundly in days," Lara interrupted. She pushed her onyx locks behind her sculpted shoulders and revealed a vial containing one of Amora's murky serums. "Don't try to fight us," the voluptuous maiden ordered after she started a gradual march towards the retreating target. The soul-forge snickered when she watched Wing trip over his own feet and land on his back. "The stress has made you weak," she continued after taking the opportunity to pin him to the worn wooden boards. Alsyne held McCallister's head to the ground with her palm and slyly ripped the cork from the flask with her thumbnail. "If you think that we're not going to protect you, then it has also made you stupid."

"Keep it away from me!" the cadet yelled as he squirmed wildly, but the broadsword simply anchored her knees about his torso and ignored the pleas. She shoved the opening of the bottle into his mouth, listened to the scraping of his heels against the timbers, and frowned when he plugged the tube with his tongue. Wing's cheek twitched and his nostrils flared from the medicine's bitterness. He refused to swallow the fluid and kept attempting to sit up until the terror projected by his distraught expression and reflexive coughs made the duo doubt their actions.

"Stop it," Luky's voice rang throughout the enclosure. Her short exclamation was sweet music to Wing's ears. Immediately, Lara pulled him up by his scruff, retrieved the filled container from his lips, and moved to let the princess take her spot. Marrok swiftly plucked the potion from the weapon's slender fingers and knelt by her inamorato. "I already know," she explained as she stroked McCallister's chest, "that you died for me."

The soldier blushed from his lady's words and leaned back on his hands for additional support. "You do?" he stuttered in response before his vest was removed by the inquisitive Lukainy. He melted beneath affectionate rubs that relaxed the muscles in his neck. How lucky was he to be blessed by such a graceful touch – one that could cocoon his despair and leave buds of ecstasy?

Cobalt veins overwhelmed Luka's ashen annuli for Wing's misery stoked her curing embers. As she set the vial aside, the noble tried to imagine what deeds could scare her brave guardian. Hidden in the luster cast by sweat and heat, ghostly outlines of metal bits and glass daggers revealed themselves to Luky. She caressed his bare skin and watched his tension swell every time an appendage passed over a region stabbed by distress. From a pouch sewn into her robe, she shyly retrieved the two trinkets meant for her familiar: a studded hide collar with a locking latch and an opulently crafted silver key.

"I think you need a reminder that you're mine," the sovereign proceeded as she tagged her guard with another accessory. Embarrassed, Wing gulped and rapidly tapped the planks upon which he sat. Mesmerized by the delicate mitts that played with tufts of his disheveled black hair, the teen focused on the lecture his mistress provided. "Also, you're still alive and you're still with me." She paused to massage his biceps and cunningly clasped his wrists before guiding them to her waist. She smiled, for it was clear that his worries were surrendering to her nursing gift.

After pitching the key into the forge's fire, Marrok planted her ear against his sternum, drove his back to the floor, and recorded the percussion tab that testified on behalf of his creedence clearwater revival. Providence's fortunate son lost himself in her beauty. Her sentences became parables – new creeds – that he could cherish until his second demise. "I need you," she cooed, "to sleep and dream with me."

McCallister had already grasped the elixir by the time Lukainy completed her request. He downed the brutal blend and squinted when he could not resist his infirmity. His eyelids became unfathomably heavy, and he toiled to stay awake long enough to deliver one last utterance. "Only if I can dream of you…"

Book 2 – Episode 14

Scabs of dried earth, tired of the union with D's myrtle wears, abandoned cloth to join the October gusts that poured over the broken walls of the Mahina Chapel. The paladin's emerald encrusted spheres photographed the sketches of devastation that bandaged the foundation of human remains. Most of them meant little to the Enchantment Flame. He could tell that they depicted precision weapons centuries ahead of his time and that no amount of study would bring them into this world. Instead, he peeled a cluster of promising parchments from the grave construct of mortared bone and thumbed through the tattered pages in search of something that would have garnered Conrad's attention. "This is what caught his eye," Alsyne whispered to the winds. "Sulfur, charcoal, and saltpeter."

"Forbidden!" The emphatic interjection towed Derrick's oculars until an outspoken companion was within the courtier's field of vision. Rusted slabs of iron hung from the man's broad frame by a chain wrapped loosely about his neck, and the theme propagated through a casing network of frayed wire belts and burnt orange plates that collectively created Kouenza's defensive shell. At nearly two and a quarter meters in height, the veteran of the Great Continental War hardly needed it; his intimidating stature was enough to make most military grunts turn tail, and those brave enough to stare into his eyes were met by a pair of vermillion cores. Trigger's frustrated blade ran his fingers through his bright brown, square-cut hair and freed an exasperated sigh. "Raiga should never have brought those abominations into our paradise."

Kouen's declaration attacked the breeze and forced it to capitulate. Wildlife – fearful of the taboo – halted their everyday activities and held still while Defy bored through the portentous looking glass. If there had been moments to spare, D would have attempted to pacify the living brand with his charm, but he feared that every second wasted was another tick Conrad gained. "Trigger did not extinguish his fire, you know? He doesn't need me around to put people under a spell, and he will use these things to get what he wants. If you know…"

Malignant beats clashed with Alsyne's melody as they were flung from Kouenza's alloy skeleton. The loyal razor had had enough. For almost two decades, he dwelled in purgatory with the other lost causes – voids that lived restlessly amongst incarcerating threads of fate. By a twisted writ, forever rammed numerous movements filled with empty notes into his psyche until all was meaningless. That lonely opus was meant to be his everlasting destiny until Trigger's aura surpassed those bland measures with a flamboyant, onyx inferno that cried for its holy extension. Through those progressive rifts, Kouen found the portal to his escape, but when he emerged, he was greeted by a punk willing to forfeit his ownership to a princess with a weak shielding flash. "For once, keep your mouth shut and listen.

"Our soil was created to be Raiga's alcove and nothing more. He came from a planet far beyond our shores to flee the indescribable cataclysms born from man's pride. He sought solitude from a reality influenced by soulless machines and compounds that smothered the spark of life, but sins know how to follow a trail. You see, Touketsu was an engineer in the Nihon Rikugan – otherwise known as the Imperial Army of Japan – and was responsible for the upkeep of those incomprehensible mechanical monsters.

"Conflicts engulfed their rock – called Terra – and millions perished in the jaws of the metal beasts. Incinerators, easily capable of duplicating Trigger's blaze, covetously churned flesh into charred caskets that needlessly asphyxiated the innocent. However, it was the twin incarnations of gluttony that bridged Raiga and Armistice. August 6, 1945 became the first day of our Continental calendar.

"In the immortal shadow of matter's decay, he found our prophetic promised land. Though, he was not alone. Amongst the lush flowers and beneath the sun and stars, companions waited to guide this soldier from the brink of heartbreak. It's a pity that Aurora and Lilith were themselves incapable of curing his ills. Yet, those three did manage to leave something behind for us to realize. Raiga named this continent Armistice for a reason; and he, the Dawn, and the Dusk made this temple from the relics of his past to send a very clear message.

"This place isn't a site to be worshiped; it's a site to be feared. It's a fucking burial ground meant to seal away the demons that you now hold and the unforgiving, detached ordnances that Conrad Wolfe von Ende der Nacht will inevitably have at his disposal." He paused, catching the twinkling honeydew crests that traversed the infinite seas of Derrick's inquisitive irides. "We're about to fall off the precipice and reshape the Mobius of brutality, but I am not surprised. I have seen this day coming since the very beginning."

"You've seen this since the very beginning?" D questioned, putting the emphasis of his verbal delivery squarely upon the adjective. It was never a good idea to interrupt Kouenza, but the verbose instrument had ranted far longer than Alsyne could allow. "That would mean that you were the one."

"Even authors misplace the meanings of their own stories," he replied in riddle. "It was foolish to think that the darkness could die while the light survived. My bainite claws may have cursed her manifestation with mortality, but the immaterial can never be struck down by our ephemeral exploits. Living, breathing in chapter after chapter, the girls will always sail between the lines as they scour the ink oceans drawn by our creators."

Quietly reflecting upon the cutter's second verse, Defy rolled into his cerebral refrain with a slew of disorderly rhythms that did not unify the parted legends of Armistice. Perhaps it was the mistake of a rambling soloist – one stuck to an emotional tempo with which history did not align – but Derrick did not believe that to be the case; Kouen selected the plural and meant it.

"You're acting like a fool," Rekkr grumbled as Wing pressed the interior lining of his cape into the razor's soaked locks. Scowling violet orbs appeared beneath the hem to capture the same hearthside gleam that projected their silhouettes onto subterranean walls. "I can take care of myself, and you should be more concerned with your own health. Incubi will spawn from Wolfe's presence if Lukainy isn't here, and it's already long past nightfall."

Standing beside the seated Daisuke, McCallister ignored his sword's complaints as he hunted concealed pockets of moisture that had appealed for asylum amongst the argent jungle. It was only after the chore was done that Wing pulled the garment from Rekkr's head and rested his chin atop his partner's sturdy crown. "You're the idiot," the teen replied before letting his palpebrae slip over worn oculars. True, without Luka at his side, Rachael would roam his subconscious unchecked as soon as he surrendered to exhaustion, but for some reason, Wing did not mind. It was because of her that he now noticed the aroma of growing fauna that piggybacked the muggy draft, heard the pitter-patter of the falling rain, and knew exactly what was important. "I'm not going to lose you again, Dai, especially not to rust."

The katana's tough exterior could not disguise the devotion that permeated his scaffolding once the cavalier gave his confession. Marrok's limbs – shot out of the psychological heavens – dropped and shook. Forgotten anamneses resurfaced, carrying with them the plethora of drawings that chronicled the friendship shared between wielder and brand and the sounds of a lonely kid that needed someone on whom to lean. *He was never meant to be here,* Daisuke concluded as Wing's arms encircled his shoulders. *He's too warm, and even now,*

I can feel him trying to hold back his worries for my sake. "It wasn't your fault..."

Rekkr stopped, unable to carry his comforting phrase to completion before the Lord of Commoners presented the burden of his full weight to the blade and its rocky throne. With his legs extended, Wing vaulted over the spiky silver tufts and dashed towards the darkness that painted the cavern entrance. Pebbles flew from the soles of the corporal's brogans to accompany the secondhand scrapings that interrupted the somber scene, and it was but a moment until McCallister's seizing hooks yanked a pair of brats from their hiding spots.

Wet clumps of black and blond fibers settled in the spaces between the guard's digits while Wing's orbs transferred his climaxing irritation to the young boys. "What are you two doing?" he shouted in a startlingly harsh tone. "Neither of you should be this close to the front!" The soundtrack crashed, its canorous theme having been stifled by a rimshot alarm that jammed the natural flow of the aural evolution. It went without saying that the knight was annoyed; with every passing bar, there were more instructions to follow and more people to defend. The last thing that he needed to do was look after a fourteen-year-old and a twelve year old squire.

Below the sinistral clutch, the 5'3" Raden W.A. Winchester fidgeted with his cherished journal and presented the newest page. The child, wrapped in fitted hide garments that transcended the medieval age, had arrived at the castle just prior to Wing's eighteenth birthday and announced that he was Raiga's apprentice. His buckled boots, skintight pants, belted gloves, and hi-col jacket were all vandalized by printed streaks of red and orange that masked his timid personality with a flaunting image. Yet his eyes, with their soft sienna annuli, always guided McCallister through the façade's labyrinth. "Practicing with charcoal," Will answered, referring to the fresh strokes that epitomized the bond shared by soul-forge and soldier.

"Epic as always," Wing commented, "but I don't buy your bullshit." He smirked, for his flattened timbre had discovered an abundance of goosebumps that were ready to tell the truth. "For starters," the protector persisted, "what could an artist possibly hope to draw on a rainy night? Second, your buddy is carrying a combat support pack, which I can't even try to justify. And finally, in case you forgot, you have your keris strapped to your back. I am not trying to question its purpose in your artistic pursuits, but it's just hard for me to see how a wavy, engraved asymmetrical dagger can help you in that regard."

Having detected the residue of a mental singularity, the partisan concentrated his interrogation upon the prisoner trussed by the opposite chirality. This subject, a scrawny runt with ceil irides, was known as TK Pachelbel. Despite his relatively puny stature and age, TK was a punk that always kept Wing on his toes. His cyan attire, patched britches, and oversized shoes masqueraded a mischievous peasant with a swindling shield that reminded the chevalier of his younger self a bit too much. The unpleasantries did not come unimpeded, though; Pachelbel was loyal to his friend and would follow Raden to the ends of Armistice if he could. He was knight-worthy material, much like the man who now peered beyond quivering orbs to search the anima. "Don't you guys get it? You could be killed out here, so just tell me what's going on."

Afraid of the consequences, TK hesitated. If telling Wing the truth meant sacrificing his relationship with Winchester, then he would have to lie to save his idol. His toes instinctively rubbed against one another as his ankles gradually swept out to lay siege to a larger base. He sniffled as sentences clogged his throat, and he held back tears by fixing his attention upon the torrential gulps that kept the betrayal at bay.

"Adventure," Raden intervened, unable to bear his vassal's predicament. "We are here because we love adventure and we want to help." The boy watched the mix of rage and disbelief wrestle for control of McCallister's countenance. "We already got yelled at by Reven and Luky! We didn't take no for an answer then, and we won't take it now! I've been waiting my whole life for this. It may not seem like a lot to you, but being able to scout for the princess is the most exciting thing that I have ever done."

The warrior exhaled, released the detainees, and dumped his cloak upon their manes. Stunned by the gear that blanketed his visage, TK howled, "Hey, what are you doing?" Like Daisuke, the children moved to dispatch the heavy veil until Wing's palms coaxed a dull stinging sensation to their jowls. He collected the drizzle droplets that chilled their youthful physiques before speaking in a strict, yet empathetic manner. "You can stay for the adventure, but if you want to stay for the legion, then you'll both have to take Trigger's entrance exam in the morning. Make sure they get to sleep," he commanded Rekkr. "Since they were scouting, Luky must be close. I'm going out to find her."

"She's awake now, you know?" Rachael teased as she paced the aisles of Wing's subconscious basilica. The spectra of violet and blue cast down from the chandeliers above portrayed Wolfe in a much different light. Scarlet gloves stretched to her elbows, and matching stockings rose from her feet to terminate mid-thigh at a yellow trim. A laced ebony corset and glittering, bejeweled shawl put the finishing touches on the sorceress's wardrobe. "You're lucky she's close," the woman commented as her wine oculars examined the cobalt beacons. "Once they go out, I can play with you as I wish."

Thorny lavender bangs hid synchromatic irides that secretly expressed levels of displeasure far greater than the caustic speech that brewed abaft his lips. "Yeah, whatever," Wing retorted from his altar-top perch. "Instead of being a bitch, why don't you try to do something useful?"

The witch sniggered at his plight and commenced her ascent towards the immaculate platform. "Feisty kitten," she purred, "I know why you're mad." She combed her lengthy sanguine strands, plucked a ferrous barb from the cruel web of memory, and brushed McCallister's hair aside to plant the gory seed that only his gaze could fertilize. "I broke you," she susurrated as her mitts straddled McCallister's knees and clasped the marble structure upon which he sat. "When you were helpless – hobbled by my snares – and drowning in my tub, you gave up."

The cadet, flustered by Wolfe's words, stiffened and loured. "There's that obstinate look," she spoke and mounted the sacred table to position herself at his side, "but all that fervor can't fool me." Rachael suspended her oral assault and chuckled. "I should give you some credit. You did last the longest, and for that, perhaps some reward is due."

Sarcasm congealed and dribbled from the paladin's orifice as skeptical coughs surfed the temple's conjured currents. "What could you possibly give as a reward?" he snapped. "Your actions depict you far better than words ever could. You can't give me a reward because you only serve your sadistic nature."

"You're probably right," the siren admitted, "but I can show you the danger; I can wake you up…"

Two seconds bridged the painful reverberations that toyed with his skull. Amora's drug had left him sluggish and confused, yet the man knew that people had gathered about his splayed constitution. They swarmed with a ferocity that overwhelmed his auditory canals, and he struggled to transpose the buzzing he heard to a key of cognizance. Their stomps jostled his nerves from the comforts of sedation and incessantly prodded each cell to pulse to the same blazing beat. For several minutes, he withstood the torments of that threshold until Lukainy's cool, soothing touch slid along his neck.

"Wake up, Wing." Her claws brushed the skin over his Adam's apple en route to the stigmatizing collar. By that very band, the royal leashed her guardian, hauled him into a seated posture, and returned him to a conscious state. From the heavy breaths and the aftershock quakes that plagued her familiar's frame, Marrok realized that her brief absence had fashioned a vulnerable aperture. "I'm sorry," she spoke with a guilt-ridden pitch that eclipsed the background's whirr.

Snatched into an apologetic hug, McCallister could not suppress his blush. Her saccharine smell stirred his olfactory nerve into a frenzy that ironically allayed his distress and expectedly hastened his arousal. Addicted, he buried his nose into her blund curls, submitted to his anatomy, and muttered a vow that only she was meant to hear. He lost himself in the midst of their amorous maze and made no effort to depart from that sanctified prison. There, the lethargic drone of their surroundings ceded to the Marcelian blur that sheathed the twosome in a band of aurum until an interrupting cough pierced the mystical shroud.

Its source – one of reality's many apparitions – lassoed the soldier's focus with incisive grey oculars, wavy blont fibers, and cocky, lighthearted vocals. "So he's the one, Lukainy? He kind of looks like a green softy to me." The man had to be in his late twenties or early thirties and had a build sculpted by years of aquatic exercise. Dressed in garbs dyed blue and black, the newcomer did not wait for the princess's response. With astounding quickness, he palmed Wing's cranium with a devastating grasp that left the teen awestruck. "Nah! I'm just shitting you, kid."

"Leave him alone, Reven!" Luka growled as her heel battered his shin. "He's already been through a lot and doesn't need to deal with additional crap from you." With her chops puffed and her brow lowered, the aristocrat kicked again for good measure.

"Ouch! When did you become such a feisty hottie? What happened to that sweet, dress-wearing girl that used to host tea parties with her big cousin?" He freed McCallister during a brief intermission and continued to torment the heir. "You should know me well enough to know that I'm just fooling around. The whole kingdom is rambling on and on about this kid and his loyalty to the king's only daughter. Do you expect me not to rib the little miscreant when he's stealing my darling relative's virginity?"

"Well, at least one of you knows how to properly treat a woman!" Marrok barked and lunged into the warrior's 80 kilogram physique. She pushed him back with her willpower alone and tried to transfer her concerns through the dilated pupils that looked down upon her crown. "He's been through a lot."

"So have you," the courtier answered, "which is why we have come as commanded." The lord looked to Wing and made his official introduction. "I am Lieutenant Reven Vallière de Marrok of the R.O.K." Pivoting, the paladin swung around to display his prized possession. Strapped to his back and engraved with the fleur-de-lis was a beautifully crafted cylinder of blackened bronze. "This is my soul-forge, Dagonet. You'll have to excuse him as he gets a little shy when he meets some new friends. Also, that grouchy-looking snowcap over there," he said, referring to a similarly dressed companion that had avoided the rest of the crowd, "is Lieutenant Cain Zedekiah Hardin."

Book 2 – Episode 15

That son of a bitch ruined everything. The internal remark sharply opposed the chorus of engineers that argued around the Führer. They were indirect, indecisive, bumbling idiots that wasted his time on ideals instead of results. His plan had been perfect and absolute. Trigger would have been removed from the equation by an act of aggression that would have toppled the peace between Cartheim and Tistal, and Lutti would have been his for the taking.

Don't you want to know how he did it, Conny? The pompous ode wired his jaw shut and ruptured molars with spikes of rage that screeched to the obnoxious tune of the Battle Blaze. He was the enemy that needed to be taken into account. He was arrogant son of Aurora that had mocked his existence from the very beginning. He was the one that was supposed to be dead!

Gloves groaned from the anger that Ende der Nacht shoved into his fists. Fed by jealousy and greed, strained tendons maintained the grasp while Conrad scrambled to prepare the next offensive move. His sister and her band of ruffians had failed to get the job done, but the male Wolfe could not blame the 7th for this defeat. There was something else – a single oversight in his computations – that gave Trigger's juvenile taunts their sting. The master manipulator had made a fatal assumption that had doomed his mission from its start; Wing did not lack powers of his own.

In that chamber, a pair of enigmas dueled for supremacy. One, secluded by psychotic sheaths sewn from threads of wrath and envy, finally emerged from its shell to decipher the other. Two decades ago, Trigger was unable to completely sever the bond between Defy and the overlord. That desperate attack, a backfiring effort meant to banish Conrad, merely delayed Wolfe's meteoric rise, but this time, something had changed. The familiar hue of the Battle Flame's inferno was no longer comatose. It had been joined with an animate amethyst touch – the aura of the Soul.

The emperor released a wearied sigh that compelled the scientists to rest. *Is it really that obvious?* Wolfe pondered, peering blankly at the documents that had been swept from the Mahina Shrine. *He didn't fail on his own. He failed because the cross required that a higher toll be paid. Trigger couldn't have been bound to his brat by chance, and neither could have Lutti.* Green irides, hidden behind swaying celestial bangs, suddenly bathed in the wonders of an epiphanic spring.

"Let's pick the things that can be mass-produced, gentlemen," he directed the staff. "We need something that every soldier can carry into battle. We need a weapon that will drop our enemies with the pull of a trigger." *How ironic.* Fingers that had never worked an honest day massaged the silky foundation of Ende der Nacht's charming countenance. "And – of course – we need a powerful device to support our forces.

"Research the compound mixtures listed in the notes and manufacture the designs marked musket and cannon." He paused to re-baptize the minions with his enchanting fire and continued emphatically, "I don't care how many resources you need. Get the job done before the thaw and guarantee a Hapsburg victory." That was all that mattered. The enveloping stately décor, royal lifestyle and abundant riches meant nothing to Conrad. Greed had long since erased such sights from his world. To him, there was but a dark, ever-expanding universe that grew solely to accommodate his unbridled conquest; in it, the only source of light was the emerald pyre that illuminated his ultimate prize.

The muscles that upholstered Wing's orbital bones twitched while his brain worked vigorously to update the stored definition of abrasive. Numerous additional synonyms accompanied the phrases that flew from Cain's mouth, but the one that stuck the best was annoying smartass. Since his introduction, the white-haired giant had done nothing but grill McCallister. "Only an idiot would sacrifice a prime soul-forge," he continued coldly. "And to hear that you did it in the heat of battle just proves that you cannot be trusted alone with the princess. You are completely incompetent."

The congregation hushed itself as the echo of Zedekiah's strike rang from the teen's frayed nerves. Prophecies were no longer required, and hidden clues buried amongst five strikes were no longer needed to justify the transposition. Trigger's runes lit the back of his fist while amber eyes launched shooting stars to down Cain's self-inflated rapture. The Battle Flame brushed Reven aside before making his way towards the heckling lieutenant. "And I'm getting tired of incompetent brats who are incapable of remembering who the fuck I am.

"Just look at you," Trigger continued. "You make it too fucking easy. For starters, if Wing was doing such a terrible job at protecting the princess, then why weren't you here years ago to perform those duties? Oh right, it's because your father was still calling the shots for you. Don't even try to pull this shit thinking that I forgot how the R.O.K. works. That service title passes down to first born, which means that, just like most people around here, you are a rich ass prick who didn't even earn what he has."

Tremors stirred the behemoth's colossal mitts as frustration coaxed the 230 pound, blue-eyed beast to flirt with the handle of his oversized war hammer. Like Dagonet, Cain's nadziak was a secondary soul-forge that was created from the scrap material leftover from the formation of the primary blades. Its large, sledge-like crown spiraled into a boar's tusk, and its shaft – a wrought iron helix that coded Hardin's fury – rose from the deathly base to meet its companion's touch.

"Go ahead and swing it, knight," Trigger taunted. "I want you to lift Kex the Boar and try to take my head with it. But before you get the chance, I will put an aurablist straight through it and shatter that fucking pig into a million pieces. The sad thing is that I doubt you'll feel the same way Wing feels about Daizer. You'll claim that you were a victim of circumstance because you treat your partner like a tool. Wing may be an annoying shit at times, but at least he knows what a soul is worth. At least he'll do what it takes to get Dai back; the question is, once your pride leads to the death of your weapon, will you?"

The six-foot-seven Zedekiah lowered his head to confront Trigger's fevered orbs. Ignoring the man's mountainous stature, the cocky paladin responded to Cain's icy countenance with a smug look that put an exclamation point upon the encounter. The Blaze stood mere inches from Hardin, yet Trigger appeared unconcerned. He could sense the unpolarized aggravation that pulsed unchecked between the lieutenant's broad shoulders and beneath his chiseled pectorals.

He loved it. In the pit of his essence, he wanted to see Cain snap. The trash-talk towards Wing was stagnant and pretentious, much like the bastard himself. He was the personification of a pompous peak, one that perceived itself as the majestic flagship of an endless range, with medals pinned by glistening snow that topped a tanned, rugged exterior. Trigger would simply wait for the volcano to blow.

From just beyond the barn's door, a methodic clap could be heard. Its steady pops shifted the setting's focal point until a strong baritone clutched the scene's reins. "I'm glad to see that you have faith in him, Wick," the man spoke as hide-bound fingers curled around the corner of the wooden board. Expecting the inevitable to drift from speculation to fact, Trigger maintained his stare. There was only one person that called him by that name: a childhood friend that was more like a brother, a comrade and his general. "It's also good to know that you still haven't learned what tact is."

"Stuff it Brigs!" Trigger barked as the gate swung open. Nearly eighteen years bled through the threshold's expanse when the Battle Flame locked onto the man's brown cores. Like a reaper revisiting his wanderers, the traveler cloaked his frame with clothes of midnight shades. A cavalier's cap of similar pitch partially covered the aphotic thatching that spilled over the heavy coat. Whiskers dotted his cheeks and chin, and a strand of golden straw that jutted from his lips colored his persona. Below the outer garment, buckles and belts pinned dyed cotton threads to his torso while wrinkled cylinders of leather shielded his legs.

Between Reven, Lukainy, Amora and Ashton, whispers surfaced that harbored hints of the newcomer's identity. His resemblance to Wing was striking, and the exposed familiarity with Trigger drew greater amounts of gossip. Lara was the first to point out the secondary strapped to the stranger's waist – a brilliant, holstered piece that had come from another era. It had been a gift from Trigger to the man's father and carried the name Ector the Magnum. The knight could almost hear Kouenza screaming in his ear for recreating one of Terra's idols, but this 357 fired of an entirely different caliber. Just as he had done for Sparks, Ector would protect its owner using fragments of the Battle Flame's own inferno.

Relegated to the sidelines, Cain incubated his wrath until the virus reached its critical phase. He would not resign himself to work with a weakling who let emotional attachments influence judgment. Yet, when the lieutenant chastised the cadet, Trigger sheltered the boy and had to interrupt. Of course, the hotheaded warrior was not intelligent enough to notice that Wing's past was irrelevant the instant that second slipped away. He had to humiliate the voice of reason instead of bitching at McCallister for failing his princess. Hardin would follow his marching orders; if Wing needed to be smothered, then Zedekiah would crush him.

Now, there was another obstacle in his way: a scruffy vagabond in his forties that stole the spotlight. "Who the hell are you, geezer?" Cain yelled, practically foaming from the lips as he demanded the answer.

The prairie grass in the traveler's mouth bobbed with each collected breath. Anger was unnecessary at the current juncture, for Brigs knew that there was plenty of time to mold the new generation – *to guide the lines of fate.* "I've looked forward to this moment," he replied to the lieutenant, "so I will ask you to hold your tongue." The others watched as the man shyly approached Wing's possessed form and hugged his friend in a loving embrace. It was obvious to those in attendance that it was more than a reunion between old pals; it was a meeting destined since the Battle of Cartheim. "To answer your question, I am Brigadier General Jack McCallister, and this is my son."

The children had passed out curled up in one another's gears, and Reven kept a close watch on the pair from a nearby earthen cradle. From the cave dwelling, one could make out Daisuke's and Kouenza's voices as they talked under stars just beginning to appear behind breaking clouds. At their feet, Dagonet scampered, unafraid of the sloppy ground that painted his fur. The loyal mortar seemed quite harmless in his fox form, and Rekkr could not help but smile at the little guy's jovial nature. Their responsibilities usually kept the weapons apart; moments like these – when they could bond beyond the battlefield – needed to be cherished.

Inside, Lukainy had fallen asleep in Wing's lap. Draped by a standard-issue R.O.K. mantle, the royal huddled against her prince and shared the bounty of her warmth. Her knees straddled his thighs, and her forearms found their homes between her bosom and his chest. Her head rested atop McCallister's shoulder, where each one of Luka's breaths could envelope his collared neck in a blanket knit for her one and only. With her presence foiling the chill that seeped from the cavern's wall, Wing floated through his thoughts.

It was an understatement to say that things were different now. Enemies that once stood in his way were now his closest supporters. The one he was chosen to protect acquired the ambition to protect him. He recalled her struggle to garner Kouen's respect as well as the incessant training that followed. When things settled, the noble performed at a level that existed only in his dreams, yet she still leaned against his body and entrusted him with her wellbeing.

It was love: life's facet that remained logically illogical. Once upon a time, it paired with random chance – as if scripted – to bring them together. It flourished in years when the whole world appeared to be a foe, and it put up with all of his flaws. It held the faith when they doubted the book itself. It persisted through sorrow to find joy, and it planted their little reason. "I'm proud of you," Wing quietly told his slumbering healer, "and I'm grateful that you are the foundation of my family."

The corporal absent-mindedly gazed at the orange, hearthside hue that polished Marrok's cheek. Tucked underneath the sturdy shell of muscle and bone that served as Luka's bed, erosive currents whirled about the concept of family. One was supposed to have relatives. The norms of society decreed it almost every second of every day, and to everyone else, family was a simple notion.

For Wing, such luxuries were never coupled to simple matters. He spent ten years living in a tiny, one-room shack in the city of Cartheim, and in those days, no one understood him or attended to his needs. McCallister cringed and shoved the lie from the banks of his consciousness. Kit had always tried his best to be a good substitute dad. Eventually, Daisuke and Trigger became his pseudo-siblings – the band of brothers. Ereint and Jeanine, the strict godparents, gave him a wonderful home, and Lukainy taught him how to share his heart.

Now, he had a family and all the complexities that came with it. He had navigated the awkward first impressions, his feelings regarding Luka's troubles, and the pains of rejection. However, the memories endured and each anxiety-inducing scar recited its own tale. In the blink of an eye, he became a brother. Jeanine's departure coincided with his mother's arrival, and within days of learning about Ereint's death, Jack McCallister had returned. One second separated Wing the orphan from Wing the son.

"And this is my son." The phrase hauled Trigger to the confines of the great cathedral and thrust Wing into the arms of his father. The ochre glaze dissolved from the teen's irides the moment McCallister regained control. Tension fastened its hold upon the cadet, sent infectious pulses throughout his extremities, and prompted an inquisitive hum from Jack. Adventure, history, pride, regret, joy, misery and more evaporated from the stranger's skin to sneak through Wing's senses.

"Son?" Finally overwhelmed by the altered state of the smithy's atmosphere, the paladin pushed away from his dad's embrace and peered into the brigadier's oculars. Staring into a visage that could have been the reflection of his own future, Wing lost his breath. The barn was banished to those swirling tides that fought to drown confusion, but everyone and everything had an alibi.

Dai loitered silently atop his oak slab; Cain, agitated by the Battle Flame, stood at his side as if ready to strike; and Luky was still in his corner. The others, caught in the spell cast by J.P. Leondegrance

McCallister, looked bewildered. His father had been alive the whole time. He was real, and after nearly eighteen years of practicing parenting from afar, he came too.

Guilt began to drive the protagonist into shock as images of Lukainy's sadness anchored amidst the torrents. *How am I supposed to react? What am I supposed to say? What am I supposed to do?* He could not even turn to gaze into Marrok's eyes. He was terrified that somehow he would make her cry again, and the thought transformed his own tears into rain. He could not even remember the number of times he wished for something like this to happen, and now, it was sinful to want it.

"I know it's a lot to take," Jack responded, "and I'm sure it will take a while. There is a lot to do, much to discuss, and a few more introductions to make. We'll get there one step at a time."

The hinges on the barn's gate squeaked when a young spy tried her best to spot her target without being detected. *He's crying*, the fourteen-year-old noted. She did her best to ignore the publicity that escorted her protruding auburn cores and black curls. *I wonder what we'll talk about. I wonder what he's thinking and what he feels like.* She stopped; her theory train derailed when his stare captured her attention.

Wing knew her, though he did not know how or why. The quakes that afflicted his imagination surrendered to this angel, for she was reality's belated gift. He felt comfort's resurgence as he peered past her pupils and pondered the possibility that perhaps her presence meant something far greater than he could comprehend. Her uncovered smile repaired the crumbled path to a land long lost, and as the first lilac shard reshaped the color of his ocular annulus, Wing called her name. "Laura."

~Welcome back Sis~

www.ingramcontent.com/pod-product-compliance
Lightning Source LLC
Chambersburg PA
CBHW020248150626
46552CB00020B/662